MW00414786

ALSO BY ISABELLA THORNE

CONTENTS

ALMOST PROMISED

Almost

Promised

Temperance

The Baggington Sisters

Isabella Thorne

A Regency Romance Novel

Almost Promised ~ Temperance
The Nettlefold Chronicles ~ The Baggington Sisters

2019 Mikita Associates Publishing

Published in the United States of America.

www.isabellathorne.com

1

---

*M*iss Temperance Baggington stared up at the sign as it threatened to free itself from its brackets and fly away upon the windstorm that was whipping its way through the streets of Upper Nettlefold.

"You have brought the devil of a storm with you?" a feminine laugh came from the street behind her and startled Temperance from her pondering.

She turned to look upon the woman whose namesake the sign declared, Mrs. Cordelia Hardcastle, owner and proprietor of Hardcastle House. She stepped through the gate and beckoned that Temperance follow. The woman was used to strange ladies landing upon her doorstep. Temperance recalled that, Mrs. Hardcastle often took on waifs and gave aid and employment to those in need. Mrs. Hardcastle's prickly demeanor hid a soft heart and kind spirit.

"Come, come," Mrs. Hardcastle called as she hastened her unidentified arrival up the step and through

3

the door. "The entire town has hunkered down for the storm. We've no reason to linger before it releases its fury upon us."

Temperance offered a thankful nod from beneath her hood and did as she was bid. It had been years since she had last set foot upon the streets of Upper Nettlefold. Five long years, to be exact. The foyer looked just as she recalled when she had raced to Mrs. Hardcastle on that last and final day, seeking salvation.

The woman had helped her then. Temperance was certain that she could count on a warm cup of tea and a room for the night; at least until she worked up the courage to do what she must. Even now, she was not certain that she should have come. The prospect of returning to her family home, after all of these years, was daunting. Of course, the object of her trepidation was no longer in residence. Her father was gone from the earth. She cautioned herself to not speak ill of the dead, but she could not quell the ill thoughts. She whispered a prayer of penitence. Five years spent with the good sisters of the Halthurst Abbey had taught her patience, but the good sisters could not quite instill humility. Nor could they take away the stain her father's brutality had left in her.

Mrs. Hardcastle called for the cook, who relieved the proprietor of the overflowing basket of goods that she carried upon her arm. Mrs. Hardcastle waved Temperance into the sitting room and requested the aforementioned tray of tea and biscuits to be brought. Sensing her companion was not yet prepared to reveal her identity Mrs. Hardcastle waited until they were alone before she shed her cloak and held out her hand to accept Temperance's to hang.

Temperance hesitated. She took a deep breath before easing the fabric of the hood away from her face. The resounding gasp was not unexpected, though it did little to settle her nerves.

"Good Lord, Miss Baggington," Mrs. Hardcastle crossed herself and asked forgiveness. "Oh, I beg your pardon Sister Temperance, you would be now, or did you take a saint's name for your own, Sister?"

"Not at all, Mrs. Hardcastle." Temperance muttered. "I am no nun. I found I could not complete the vows, though I will ever be thankful for your facilitation of my acceptance into Halthurst Abbey."

Mrs. Hardcastle clucked at Temperance to hand over her cloak so that it might be hung to dry. "Not another word until we've sat proper," she instructed. "I should say we'd best start at the beginning."

"Yes, Ma'am," Temperance obliged. She had no belongings save the thick woolen sheath dress that covered her thin frame and a paper-wrapped bundle that she settled beneath a nearby bench. The Abbey kept its own flock from which to make the woolen cloth. Temperance had grown used to the coarse fabric after all these years. She had nearly forgotten what a muslin gown might feel like against her skin. She recalled a fine silk and velvet blend that her mother had commissioned from London before she had made her escape. Temperance had worn it once, on the evening she had been made to meet the gentleman that she had been promised to marry. The gown had been a dream; the gentleman, a nightmare. Temperance shuddered with the thought.

"Oh my dear, you are chilled," Mrs. Hardcastle said misjudging the reason for her tremors.

Just as the tray was delivered, the storm let loose with a vengeance. Mrs. Hardcastle moved to the window to pull the curtains shut against the draft.

"There now," she clapped her hands. "No need to let the dreary outside spoil the inside. I must admit that you were the last person I expected to see upon my doorstep."

"Yes, well, in the light of... recent events..." Temperance trailed off. She did not know how to say the words over the lump that had just appeared in her throat. She felt as if she might choke on it. Mrs. Hardcastle took note of her guest's discomfort and moved to pour the tea so that Temperance might take a moment to recover. Temperance took a long draught on the scalding liquid and found that the warmth that trailed down her throat and through the center of her body did give her strength.

"With recent events being as they are," she continued, "I thought I might attempt a visit."

"Yes," Mrs. Hardcastle nodded. "I assume you are referring to the death of your father, the Viscount Mortel. Strange thing, that," she said with a vague nod into her own cup. "It came on so sudden. Had I known you had not taken your vows I would have written straight away."

"I tried," Temperance explained. "Again and again, I tried. It never did seem right. I could not do it."

Mrs. Hardcastle pierced Temperance with a reprimanding look. "What didn't seem right? Taking the vows or writing to your family?"

Temperance lowered her head and whispered. "I couldn't. What if he..."

Mrs. Hardcastle interrupted. "Your family seems to think it done, and you made a proper member of the Abbey," she scolded. "Have you not written to them in all these years? Not even to your sisters?"

Temperance shook her head. "I asked the Mother Abbess to burn their letters. She didn't, of course. She kept them with the hope that I might ask for them one day, but I could not bear it. It was better to have a clean cut else I might have been tempted to return for my sisters' sakes."

"Do not go on feeling badly about that," Mrs. Hardcastle instructed. "I can see that you do. You have no reason for such self-infliction. You were right to think of yourself for once. Those years of trying to shelter your siblings only made it worse for you. You could have never kept him from the others once they came of age; especially not once you had been married off to that brainless oaf."

"I thought it best that everyone think I only wished to avoid my marriage," Temperance hung her head as she recalled the frightened child she had once been. She was still frightened, only less of a child.

"It was long ago," Mrs. Hardcastle soothed.

"But I remember like it was yesterday," she whispered. "I preferred to keep the rumors to my own name, rather than burden the family. Still," she shuddered, "I knew when Father said I was to marry his old friend that I would never be free of him...of either of them. They had some sort of...

arrangement, I suspect, to... because Father did not want to lose..."

Mrs. Hardcastle swore under her breath. She was not one prone to profanity and so the effect was all the more significant to express her disgust.

"My blood still boils as much as that first day you told me of your troubles." The older woman bit into a biscuit with a vengeance. "Curse your father and may he rot below. Never was there a gentleman who deserved eternal flames more than he."

Temperance agreed, though she had yet to be so vocal in her opinions as the independent Mrs. Hardcastle. The good sisters would never allow such. The abbess had indeed told Temperance to pray for her father's soul. She had attempted to do so, but she could not help thinking he deserved damnation for the hell he visited upon his own daughters. Still such thoughts should not creep into prayers.

"I promised you he would not get away with it forever," Mrs. Hardcastle nodded. "I will not lie. I paid a visit to your mother after your departure and plied her with some of my homemade wine. She missed you terribly but was relieved to know that I had sent you someplace safe. Well, she was well into the bottle when she finally spoke of the matter herself."

"She told you?"

Mrs. Hardcastle nodded.

Temperance hung on to her every word. She had not spoken to her mother since the day that she ran away without warning. All that had happened since was news to her. "What did she say?" Temperance asked.

"I've never seen a lady more like a fountain than the Viscountess Mortel. I suspect years of holding in the pain came forth at once." Mrs. Hardcastle clucked once more. "Of course she knew I could be trusted, just as you knew. Still, she was terribly afraid of him, with reason. Afraid for herself and her children, she was. She was happy you were free but her hands were tied with the other girls. She knew she had to get the rest of them out of the manor, so she threw herself into the marriages. That did not work out so well for Miss Prudence, but there was naught to be done, what with her having been caught in an embrace. At the time, I thought it a blessing. Prudence would be quickly married and away from the Viscount. Her new husband being an earl meant that her father, as a lesser member of the peerage, could not touch her. Of course, that was before I started asking questions as to the nature of the Earl of Fondleton. I can tell you this: I did not like what I discovered. By then, it was too late I'm afraid. Lord Fondleton had some shady dealings that he kept well below the notice of proper society. A wicked rake of a man and a swindler to boot."

Temperance bowed her head and mumbled some halfhearted comment in memory of the late Lord Fondleton.

"Hold your tongue," Mrs. Hardcastle scolded. "Jasper Numbton was as bad as they come. Poor Prudence fell from one beast's trap and straight into another. Bless her poor little heart, a widow at such a young age."

Temperance nodded. "Still, it all worked out in the end."

"That it did," Mrs. Hardcastle shook her head with a

smile. Though the older lady did not know the entire story; there were few that did. It was clear that Prudence was happy to move on from the loss of her first husband. Some still called her "*the baggage*" and said a lack of decorum was expected of a woman such as Prudence, but they did not know the truth.

Desperation does strange things to a person. Temperance knew Prudence was indeed despairing when she arrived at the Abbey, bedraggled and frantic. No one could blame Prudence if they knew the true story. Prudence had mourned for the appropriate time and now it was whispered that the wealthy widow Fondleton had already made a connection to the Baron Halthaven who lived in the north. It would not be long, rumor had it, before she would be happily remarried, or at least Temperance hoped it was so. Prudence deserved happiness.

"I cannot believe that Mother told you about Father!" Temperance turned the conversation back with a look of awe. "She made us all swear never to tell a soul. It would ruin us and the family. She was certain if we told anyone, father would make a claim for *scandalum magnatum*. Isaac would lose his inheritance and the manor and... well all sorts of trouble, I'm sure. She especially did not want the boys to learn of it. I did always wonder if they had their suspicions, but we did well to keep silent. Thankfully the boys were often away at Eton, and later making visits to their friends. Besides," Temperance added, "it would not do to incite Father's wrath. He was cruel to even to my brothers though not in the same way as the girls."

The Baggington sisters were blessed with four

brothers. With the protection of their position in mind, the five daughters, along with their mother, had done what was necessary to keep the truth below the notice of the gentlemen. There was nothing that destroyed the families of the peerage faster than internal disputes. Temperance shuddered to think what Isaac, the eldest son and newly proclaimed Viscount Mortel, would have done had he known. A confrontation with his father would have had him stripped of his inheritance, title, and future without hesitation, she was sure, but he was away at school when the abuse had started and none of the women ventured to speak of it on the rare occasions Isaac visited home. The late Viscount Mortel was not above using violence to enforce his rule. His sons had walked in his shadow, doing their best to keep his approval or to keep their heads low.

"The entire situation was a mess from the off," Mrs. Hardcastle grumbled. "If I had my way..." she trailed off. "Well, let's just say the matter would have been handled sooner."

"Sooner?" Temperance asked. She was afraid to press further into the implication that it had been *handled* at all.

"The Lord works in mysterious ways," Mrs. Hardcastle smiled. "Look at Lord Fondleton, Providence sorted him out as well."

Temperance did not know how to respond. Neither Providence, nor the Lord, had sorted out the Earl of Fondleton, but Temperance kept her own council on the matter. It did not take much thought to realize that Jasper Numbton was long overdue for a confrontation.

Temperance would not speak on that tale, however, for there was much there that was to be kept a secret. Her own, as well as her sister's.

"Now," Mrs. Hardcastle continued without pause, "does your family know of your return?"

"No," Temperance admitted. "I was hoping that I could stay here until I work up the courage to make myself known to them."

Mrs. Hardcastle shook her head and pursed her lips. "I am full to bursting at the moment," she explained. "I had to pair up some of my girls. Even if I had the room, you know what I would say…"

Temperance nodded. Mrs. Hardcastle could always be relied on for firm and fair advice. Temperance had wondered if she would turn her away from the start. It was Temperance's own indecision that was keeping her here when there was more than enough room at the manor. She kept reminding herself, her father was no longer there to darken the doorway. The thought made her feel rather giddy.

"Chin up, child," the boarding house matron said with a bolstering grin. "You've no one left to fear anymore."

"I know…" Temperance worried, "but shall they accept me?" She had run away without a word, without correspondence for five long years. If it had not been for the recent arrival of her sister Prudence at the Abbey Temperance might have never spoken to her family again. The knowledge of her father's passing had changed everything. In that moment, she had finally felt hope.

"For heaven's sake child," Mrs. Hardcastle laughed. "You lived in a religious institution for five years. Have you not heard the story of the prodigal son?"

"Of course I have," Temperance replied.

"Then you know that you shall be welcomed home again with open arms," the elder woman advised. "And if they do not accept you; then you come back to me, and I will give them all a piece of my mind!"

Temperance could not help but laugh at the rock of strength that was Mrs. Hardcastle. There were rumors that she had once had a tragic history of her own, though no one knew the exact nature of the tale. Still, whatever had happened had built an iron resolve in the woman that left her without fear. Temperance wished that one day she might be as confident as her benefactress.

Though she still trembled with nerves at the thought of meeting her family after five years, Temperance began to feel encouraged by Mrs. Hardcastle's confidence. They agreed that Temperance would stay through dinner, to wait out the storm, and then the boarding house driver would take her along the winding road to Mortel Manor which lay well outside the bustling town of Upper Nettlefold.

2

The storm did not let up before nightfall. By then, Mrs. Hardcastle had rearranged the rooms so that Temperance might have one of the minuscule maid's quarters for her own. It was little more than a closet, but Temperance did not mind.

"I wish I could offer more, but this will have to do on short notice. Fanny can share a bed with her sister for the night and there's no other way too it. I'll not reduce my establishment to ladies sleeping on the floor." Mrs. Hardcastle said with a curt nod.

Temperance had promised that she was in no need of a bed, only a place to rest her tired eyes. In the Abbey, the sisters had often slept on little more than stuffed pallets on the ground. Not that the Abbey could not have afforded more, but the sisters prided themselves on the enactment of poverty and refused to improve their situation in the slightest. All funds were directed toward those who were truly in need. Temperance had not had a proper bed in five years. The servant's quarters would be like a lavish estate. She informed the owner of the boarding house as much and received nothing but a horrified scowl in response.

"We can do better than that," Mrs. Hardcastle promised with renewed determination. Temperance laughed as she declined a scented bath, and a cold compress for her travel-weary head to soften her thoughts before she fell into her dreams.

"I do not want to be any trouble. I shall simply wash in the basin. However, I would beg an extra candle to read by," she replied.

"Will you still study the Scriptures now even though you have decided against taking the cloth?"

Temperance shook her head. "I think I have read enough of that for the time being," she laughed.

Mrs. Hardcastle looked suspicious but did not press the issue. "Alright then, a basin of water and an extra candle if you wish."

Temperance thanked the matron and even accepted one of the rarest gifts of all, an embrace from the rigid lady.

"I am glad to see your face again, Miss Baggington," Mrs. Hardcastle whispered into Temperance's ear. "You always deserved better than your plight. Now, you just might have the chance to live as you would choose."

"I am not sure what it is that I want anymore," Temperance admitted with a shrug. "I have no grand expectations or fanciful dreams of finding a handsome gentleman. I only wish to exist in peace. That would be enough for me."

"That is a good place to start," Mrs. Hardcastle agreed. "Only promise me that you will not settle into obscurity. I have said it before, and I will say it again. You were made to enjoy something much more. Do not shy away from happiness, my dear. You have had enough misery. It is time you grasped life with both hands."

Temperance was not sure what sort of happiness Mrs. Hardcastle was referring to. If she meant that of a gentleman's attentions, as most women did, then she had missed her mark. Temperance shook her head. Mrs. Hardcastle was, as far as Temperance was aware, a widow. She had never needed a man to stand upon her own two feet. No, Temperance did not think that Cordelia Hardcastle was the kind of woman to imply that a lady needed a gentleman to be happy. However, she was right in some small way. Perhaps Temperance would need to work a little harder to find happiness again. What that meant, she was not sure.

Temperance made her way to her sleeping chamber, which was little more than a bed squeezed in beside the smallest side table that Temperance had ever seen. It was just large enough to hold the basin and candle that she had been provided.

She washed in the basin and when it seemed that the rest of the house had gone to sleep, Temperance pulled her knees up into the borrowed nightie. She leaned against the wall for support, the flattened pillow protecting against the hard wooden boards of the wall. From beneath the bed, where she had placed it earlier in the evening, she pulled the paper parcel.

The package stared at her, from the middle of the

bed. Its small, inoffensive form belied the terror within. For, wrapped beneath the protective layer, and secured with a cross of twine, were five years' worth of letters from her family. Some might bring her happiness, others might renew horrors that she had longed to forget. She would not know until she set eyes upon them.

Sister Beatrice, the Mother Abbess of Halthurst Abbey, had told Temperance that the moment she confronted the contents of these letters, she would begin an integral part of her healing. She did not know if she believed the nun, but she had promised to read them just the same.

"I never did expect you to stay," Sister Beatrice had revealed on the day that Temperance took her leave from the Abbey for good. "You always gazed out the windows, as if you longed to venture out, but were afraid to do so. I told your sister Prudence that these walls were not meant to hide one from the world. I meant that," she had said. "I allowed you to stay because I thought you needed the peace. While your father was alive you could never exist in the world outside of our walls. Prudence could have. She wanted to be away and to start a new life. I knew that you could not move forward until the past was resolved. I sensed that you were only biding your time. However many years that would be... I was not certain. Perhaps a lifetime. Now, I believe the time has come. You have been given a fresh start, an opportunity that should not be wasted. You are not made to be a nun, I think we both knew that from the beginning. You are a good girl, but you do not have the calling. Nonetheless, this has been your home for five years now. Like any true home, you shall always be welcome and well-received. We are thankful for what time you shared with us."

Temperance had promised to visit on occasion. Sister Beatrice was right. She had found a new sort of family in the Abbey: one that would always be a part of her. The sisters, the novices and the postulants had all said their tearful farewells and wished Temperance good fortune and blessings on her new path. She had tucked the letters of her past beneath her arm and set out into the wild unknown toward what was once her childhood home.

Now, the prospect of reading those letters seemed even more daunting than before. With a deep exhale that caused the flame of the candle to flicker, she dove in with all of the courage that she could muster.

Sister Beatrice had kept the letters in the order that they had been received and so Temperance flipped the bundle over and started from the beginning.

My Dearest Daughter,

I do not know where you have gone; only that Cordelia Hardcastle says that you are safe and she shall see to the forwarding of this letter. Though my heart aches for the loss of you, I take comfort in knowing that you are well. I have not the time to tell all. I must post this letter before your father returns. I am certain you can predict your father's response to your departure.

He and Lord Vardemere talked at length about what should be done. Lord Vardemere is determined to have you brought back. He demands your dowry as payment for his trouble and that, upon your retrieval you be handed over to his possession.

I am sorry to inform you of the loss of your dowry, though Cordelia tells me you have left for a convent and shall have no need of it. Still, your dowry should have been yours...if nothing else to give to the Abbey for your upkeep and their charitable work.

I do not write to convince you to return. You will be far safer where you are. My darling Temperance, my eldest daughter and firstborn child, I love you with all my heart.

Please, do not return. If ever there were a time when it can be managed, I shall write to you upon the wings of the wind and have you brought to my side at once. As it is, your father is young in years and virile. I am afraid that you shall be lost to me forever.

Now I must put my thoughts to Prudence's marriage. I swear I shall not be lax and allow your father his choice. Nay, this shall be mine. I am sorry that I failed you, Temperance. I suppose I shall always see you as my baby. I was taken aback when your father announced he had already accepted a suitor for your hand. I was ill prepared and too late for you, my daughter.

Nonetheless, please know that you shall always be in my heart and in my prayers.

With all my love,
Your Mother

One letter in and Temperance was already covering the pages in tears. Her mother, the Viscountess Mortel, had written only three days after Temperance's escape. Likely it had taken that long to even discover how to send a note in secrecy.

Now, she was glad for her mother's advice, but had she read the words five years ago she was certain that they would have eaten at her resolve. If only for that which was not revealed; how her siblings fared.

Temperance wiped her eyes and unfolded the next letter. Though the ache in her heart was immense, she forced herself to read each in turn.

Temperance,

Papa is cross. Mama says she can send this if we promise to keep quiet, and tell no one we have news of where you have gone. We miss you. Nobody laughs at us anymore. Nobody smiles. We wish you had taken us with you. Our tenth birthday was last month and you weren't there.

Mama says Prudence has to get married, but she does not want to. Prudence said it isn't fair and nobody likes her anyways, but she has set her sights on the Duke. She says once she marries him, she will take us all away with her because a duke can chastise a viscount. We do not think it will happen, but we are hopeful nonetheless.

We are stuck here until Prudence and Mercy are married. If only we could all be married and go away forever. If you get this, come steal us away too. We won't be a bother. We promise. We shall wait out by the old broken barn every Tuesday night when Papa is gone to play cards with Lord V. We are glad you didn't marry him. He smells like tobacco and his teeth are rotted too.

Please come for us.
Faith and Hope

Temperance's heart broke for the youngest of her sisters. She had abandoned them. She had abandoned them all. Temperance was not certain it was something that could ever be forgiven, but she had never stopped loving her sisters, despite having not come back for them. The twins had been voracious and full of life. So young when she had left, Faith and Hope did not understand her reason for haste. They would be women now. She prayed that their spirit had not been squashed in the years that followed. She forced herself to read on.

There were several letters that spoke of her father's rage at her escape. It appeared to Temperance that he had searched her out after a time and had even shown up at the convent to retrieve her. Temperance had never heard the tale, but it was clear that he was firmly rebuked. Her father assumed she had already taken her vows and that there was naught to be done for it. In his anger, he had unleashed his wrath upon pen and paper, sending it to the Abbey so that she might know what she had cost him in the useless loss of her dowry. Temperance was glad that she had never known it, and she made a mental note to thank the Mother Abbess for her protection.

Once her location was outed, Temperance's siblings and mother began to write on a more regular basis.

Her brothers updated her on their schooling and the usual correspondence. Having not known the true cause for her abandonment, their letters were less emotional that that of the females. Temperance retrieved the most details of her family's doings from her brothers. They wrote of the holidays, summer outings, and the ladies that caught their interest. If she read between the lines, she could see that her brothers spent little time at the manor. They raced away to visit friends or return to school as often as possible, so as to avoid their father's temper. It was clear that they had no idea what they were leaving their sisters to suffer. Not, Temperance reminded herself, that there was anything that her brothers could have done if they had known.

Thru five years of letters Temperance watched her family grow. When the first candle burnt too low to read by, she lit the second from the flame of the first and began anew.

Eventually, without her response, the letters trickled down from monthly notes to once or twice a year. Prudence spoke of her disgust with husband hunting, as she called it. She had been forced to practice an effected voice and wear ostentatious attire like a peacock attempting to draw in a mate. Prudence told of her frustration. Temperance was just glad that she had not been subject to such primping. Men had always noticed Temperance for her looks. She wished that they would see something more in her than the symmetry of her face or the elegant curl of her dark hair. To have her sister paraded around for men to gape at made her shiver with disgust. Of course she had heard all about it from Prudence in recent months when she too ran away to Halthurst Abbey. Had she known all of this earlier, Temperance could not say whether she would have had the strength to stay away.

Her father offered raging lines every so often. Temperance assumed that he was well into the drink. For years he swore that she should still marry Lord Vardemere, for the man had been paid her dowry. It was only after three years' worth of letters that Prudence revealed that Lord Vardemere had married a young girl of only fifteen. Temperance's person was now safe, but the dowry was still lost and never forgotten, or forgiven, by the Viscount Mortel.

The Viscountess was the only one who wrote regularly. If only a line here or there, to remind Temperance that she was in her mother's thoughts.

Temperance got the sense that her mother used the letters to talk to herself more than to her daughter. She aired her thoughts and concerns, some much too weighty to place upon the shoulders of her younger children. Now that Temperance was older she could understand the letters better than she might have when they ought to have been received. Either way, it seemed her mother had taken to the letter writing as her one true confidant. Perhaps she had suspected that Temperance was not reading them. Perhaps she thought that they might never be read at all and so she could pour out her soul.

Mercy, the quietest and most reclusive of all the Baggingtons seemed to bear the heaviest brunt of Temperance's departure. She had already been their father's second favorite before Temperance had made her escape. Prudence had held less appeal to their father, for whatever reason. Temperance thought she had grown into a fine looking woman. Perhaps it was that she was softer than the others, more buxom and full-figured. The twins shared a room which was a blessing of sorts as it limited the Viscount's boldness. So it was that Mercy became the next favorite. She never said as much, but Temperance sensed her withdrawal through the choice of her words. Temperance and Mercy had once clung to one another for support. It was to this sister that Temperance felt that she owed the most. Mercy had always been strong of heart and mind, though understandably cold when it came to her emotions. Temperance wondered what sort of woman she had become and if the ice of her heart had settled, to be frozen forever.

When the Viscount died, her mother had written. Nothing more than a pair of lines;

> *Your father passed yesterday. I wish I could bring you back to me but I cannot fault your devotion.*

> *With my unending love,*
>   *Your Mother*

With the thought that her daughter had made her full commitment to the pious life of the Abbey, her mother had resigned herself to the fact that Temperance would never return. Still, she had written to let her know, as promised, as soon as the moment had arrived.

Isaac would be made Viscount now and her mother the Dowager Viscountess. It still seemed strange to think that their father was gone. He had always seemed too large for life. Undefeatable. Something dark that would always lurk in the back of her mind.

She could not imagine their home without him. The walls themselves had grown darker with his moods. It was as if he had the power to call up the fires of hell with his fury and his tempers had raged just as often as the English rain.

By the time Temperance turned to sleep, the servants were beginning to move like scampering mice about the boarding house. Soon, the first light of the sun would shine through the windows. The pile of opened letters lay sprawled around her. Temperance did not care if they were crumpled. When she woke, she would burn them. Their message would remain forever imprinted in her mind.

_T_emperance waited until the morning fog had lifted. It was near to midday when she began her journey to the manor house in which she had spent, and lost, her childhood. Perhaps by noon her family would have begun their day without being set upon with a surprise first thing. She could only hope that she was well received. After the series of letters, she was less certain than before. Her sisters, at least, seemed to have struggled in her absence. Temperance was not entirely convinced that events would have been the same if had she remained. Her very presence might have protected her younger siblings. She shuddered with the thought.

The manor that had been designated to the family Mortel for several generations had once been the pride of Nettlefold proper. When her father had taken over the residence, it had slipped into obscurity. His isolationist ways, combined with the necessity of keeping his perversions secret, had caused him to withdraw his family from any more than the barest requirements of society. It was still considered one of the most beautiful manors in the neighborhood, but it was little used and never welcomed visitors. The house was massive in its expansive domain. Temperance had spent many years hidden away, discouraged from visiting the town. Many forgot that the Baggington family had once been beloved members of the community. One generation was all that it had taken to ruin their connections. One generation was all that it had taken to turn a prominent family into nothing more than what the locals referred to as "*the baggage.*" Temperance sighed with the thought. She had suffered with the nickname, but not so much as her sister Prudence.

The wagon, graciously offered by Mrs. Hardcastle, bumped along the rutted road. Long ago it had been the passageway to hundreds of guests each year. Now, it served as little more than a service road.

"Sorry, Miss," the driver called. "The Lord Mortel is having the road filled so it's a little shifty at present. It shall settle into a nice path in time."

Temperance's head shot out the window before the man had finished his sentence. The Viscount was repairing the road?

It took her a moment to recall that the Viscount Mortel was now her brother, Isaac. Of course he would repair the road. Isaac had always been meticulous in his ways. Top of his class at Eton and brilliant to the point of baffling his counterparts, he often planned many years in advance for whatever goal he set to achieve. He would make a fine landholder, she thought with a smile.

The thought made her impending arrival slightly more nerve-wracking. To approach Isaac, her little brother, was one thing. Now that he was the Viscount, combined with the fact that she had not known him these five years, brought palpitations to her heart. Perhaps he had changed much in her absence. Worse yet, perhaps he now resembled their father in taste and temper. The thought caused her to shudder. At worst, she determined, she would remove herself once more. This time, she decided, for good.

At best, he was the same lovable little Isaac that she recalled: The Isaac who had picked nettles from her hair when she had caught herself in a bind. Isaac who had stood his ground as her guardian whenever he was aware that a man made a foreword advance upon her. He had darkened the daylights of one boy in town who commented on Temperance's beauty with the implication that the loveliness traveled further than her face. Four brothers had she, and all as protective as Temperance might have wished, but all her junior. Still, if they had only known that the true demon their sisters needed protecting against resided within the walls of their own house. Would they have rushed home from school to save them?

It had been five years. Isaac had been given much time in which to change. Prudence had once said that all men had only a matter of time before they gave in to the demon within them. Temperance had believed her. Yet, Prudence had recently found herself deeply in love with a very respectable and kind gentleman who had dispelled much of her previous concerns and proven himself above such base behavior.

Could their devilish father have sired gentlemen of true character? Was it even possible for his sons to be decent representations of their sex? Temperance hoped it was possible, though she was not certain that she believed it true. It was better to imagine her brothers as the boys she knew rather than the men they might have grown to be.

A small voice in her head cried at the loss of their childhood. Even if they were not as terrible as their father, it was certain that they had matured. They would have changed from the boys that Temperance had once loved. It was very possible that they too had turned cold and bitter as they came of age. She wondered if any of them had married. She had forgotten to ask. Mrs. Hardcastle had been kind enough to mention that all of the girls remained unwed as of yet. No mention of the sons had crossed her lips during their brief conversations.

Once Isaac married, his siblings would be forced from the Manor. Temperance was sure of this. A wife would not want such a large group of siblings in the house. Temperance had never stopped to think where she would go if that were the case. She had no income, or dowry, on which to rely. She did have the teachings of the nuns. Perhaps she could become a governess. The Mother Abbess would surely provide her with a reference.

Never had Temperance heart beat such an aggressive pattern. Her chest felt as though it might burst with each passing turn of the wagon wheels. Each rotation brought her closer to all that she had avoided for as long as she cared to recall. What might her family think of her? She had abandoned them all. Her hands were damp. She clenched her skirts to dry them. To no avail. Her nerves had gotten the better of her.

The carriage drew to a stop beside the wide curve of the grand marble steps.

"Shall I announce you, Miss?" the driver called down.

"No, thank you," she replied in a hurry. "I shall just knock at the door."

Temperance used to try to imagine the reception lines of the massive balls that her grandfather had hosted, but she could not bring her mind to place more than two or three people upon the step at a time. Even with nine children, the Baggington offspring tended to make themselves scarce in the main house when their father was in residence.

"Would you mind waiting until I know that I shall be received," Temperance asked with a trembling voice when she had dismounted the carriage.

The driver looked down upon her with warm eyes, as if he knew the depths of her heart and her worries.

"You'll be received, Miss," he promised, "but I shall wait just the same."

She thanked the man for his kindness, wishing that she had a spare coin or two to press into his hand. As a lady, and more so as a postulant, she had no purse. She thanked him again and he tipped his hat. With a deep breath to bolster her spirit, Temperance turned and marched straight up the steps and rapped her knuckles upon the fourteen foot tall carved doors.

The door inched open and the gaunt face that peeked out was one that Temperance knew as well as her own, save for the clouded eyes. The old butler peered at her, squinting for all he was worth, but he did not appear to recognize her.

"Mr. Gibbons!" she exclaimed.

"Excuse me, Miss?" the butler replied standing a little straighter at the sound of his name. Temperance could not believe that Mr. Gibbons was still alive. The old man had been the butler when her father was a child. He was quite ancient when she left the manor, but five years had passed and he apparently still resided at the estate.

"Oh, I did not expect you, Mr. Gibbons," she explained. "Is my brother in? Or, my mother, perhaps. Anyone, really."

Temperance grimaced. She had not planned her entrance well. In fact, she had not planned it at all. She did not know whom to ask for or call upon first. Her brother was technically the owner of the house now, and his would be the word that said stay or go, but her mother was the eldest living resident and the previous lady of the house. Temperance so wanted to see her mother and perhaps throw herself into her arms as if she were a small child.

Mr. Gibbons squinted and leaned further through the doorway as if to make out her features.

"Lady Prudence?" he asked. "My, but you look different than I recall. Your siblings are all just sat for their midday tea. Come in."

He stepped back to allow her entrance but Temperance hesitated.

"Mr. Gibbons," she said in a hush. "It is Temperance."

"Who?" he asked, raising his voice which made Temperance think he had grown a little deaf in the past five years as well.

"Temperance," she repeated rather loudly. "Temperance Baggington."

Mr. Gibbons scoffed. "I might have lost my eyesight some and a bit of my hearing but I'm not daft. Name yourself proper or I'll shut the door on you. Miss Temperance hasn't been seen by anyone hereabouts in ages."

"I assure you. It is I," Temperance urged. "I left five years ago and joined a convent, but here I stand, true as anything. My father recently passed..."

"That he did, but anyone in Nettlefold would know that news."

Temperance wracked her brain for more intimate news that would secure her entrance. "Your wife, Mrs. Gibbons, baked the very best blueberry scones and she would let me eat them hot with butter before the rest of the house was awake."

A strange look came across Mr. Gibbons' face "That she did. She were a wonderful cook," Gibbons replied, but he shook off the moment of nostalgia. "Still, anyone can answer thus if they had the wits to ask questions. I'll not believe it."

Temperance continued.

"She had a mole on her face just on the left side above her lip, and she hated wearing her cap, but would smash it on her head whenever any of the gentry would come about. She was less fastidious for me and my siblings and plied our silence with treats. My favorite was blueberry scones, but Isaac loved gingerbread, and Prudence the shortbread..."

Without thought of propriety, Mr. Gibbons suddenly grasped her face in his hands and pressed his nose nearly against her own as he looked her over.

"Miss Temperance?" he asked disbelieving. She nodded her face still held in the old man's hands. He smiled deeply and recognition filled his clouded eyes.

"I cannot believe you are returned, Miss. You're terribly skinny," he continued. "Always been a slight thing, but do they not feed you, the nuns?"

"I'm not a nun," she whispered. Mr. Gibbons had always been her favorite of all the servants. "I shall tell all later. First, I must see my family."

"Right you are," Gibbons replied. "Oh, I'll tell the cook right away. She's going to want to prepare a feast for your arrival, and I'm seeing that you need to eat lass."

"Cook?" Temperance questioned.

"My Gertrude died two summers past," he said. "God rest her."

"My condolences," Temperance replied. If she had known she would have had a Mass said for the cook's soul. She loved the woman almost as much as her own family... and in the case of her father, considerably more.

"The new Lord Mortel, your brother, replaced the old cook."

Temperance could not get used the fact that her little brother was now the Viscount.

"The one that took over my Gertrude's place in the kitchen was your father's creature...not to speak ill of the dead," Mr. Gibbons amended. "But your brother is a breath of fresh air in this house. He will be most happy to see you, Miss." He turned to announce her.

"Pray, do not be so quick," Temperance warned. "I haven't been received yet. My return might not go off as I hope."

"Oh codswallop," Mr. Gibbons laughed. He waved the carriage away which, for whatever reason, he could see just fine at the distance. "There is nothing your family is going to want more than to see you. And not a nun, after all! Land's sakes child, what have you been up to all this time?"

"Oh, I tried," Temperance laughed. "I tried to be a nun. I was not very good at it."

"You always did talk too much," Gibbons teased. "Probably couldn't keep quiet enough to hear your prayers."

Temperance giggled. She had missed the banter and the affection that existed in society outside of the pristine convent walls. Without great involvement in the Nettlefold community, the few servants that resided at the manor had established deep relationships with all the Baggington children, often protecting them from their own father. Temperance had missed them. As nice as the sisters of Halthurst Abbey had been, Mr. Gibbons was right, conversation at the convent had been sorely lacking.

She could hear a cacophony from the tea room well before she neared the door. Her father would never have permitted such raucous behavior. Silence was a virtue, he would say. To add to his flaws, the late Viscount had an obsession with the Good Book, but he manipulated the interpretations for his own ends.

"Jesse wrote that he and Simon are stationed together for the next fortnight," a light feminine voice informed the room. "I pray for any who cross their path. Let the little Frenchman beware."

"Those two could bring a town to its knees without even men to take orders," a matching tone replied.

"A funny sentiment from the pair of you," a male voice replied with humor. "If women could command armies I'd fear for any who crossed your path!"

The words confirmed that the first two speakers had been none other than the twins, Faith and Hope. Ten year old girls they were no longer. They would be fifteen now, on the verge of womanhood. Temperance could hardly bring herself to enter the tea room knowing that she could not even recognize the sound of her own sibling's voices. Had so much time passed?

Mr. Gibbons cleared his throat and gestured that she enter.

She had a moment of serious hesitation, shook her head, and took a step away from the door.

Gibbons would have none of it. Without further ado he stepped into the tea room and announced the arrival of a guest.

"We were not expecting anyone, Gibbons," the same male voice replied. Temperance determined that it must be Isaac, though the deep rumble sounded nothing like the teenage boy that she remembered.

"True enough, M'Lord," Gibbons replied. "All the same I think you will be happy for the interruption."

"Shall I adjourn to the drawing room?" Isaac said with a sigh. It was clear that he was loathe to leave his siblings. Lively afternoon meals were not a thing that Temperance recalled. It must be a highly prized tradition that had just begun.

"I think not, M'Lord," Gibbons replied.

"We've just sat to tea," the horrified voice of the Dowager Viscountess spoke. The Lady Mortel had been well trained to propriety. Old habits die hard. Her husband would have never allowed that a guest be received at the table in the middle of a meal. Knowing that her mother was so near, and yet so far, brought tears to Temperance's eyes. She refused to let them fall and muss her face. If she were to meet them, she did not want to do so with her face all blotchy and red.

"I think it shall be just fine," Gibbons replied with a grin.

Temperance wanted nothing more than to back away, but Mr. Gibbons had already announced a guest and was beckoning her forward. She could not race away now. There would be questions and then she would be made a fool.

Before she entered the room she scowled at Gibbons. Despite his strained eyesight he seemed to catch her point, for the look was met with a hardy laugh in response.

"Who is it, Gibbons?" one of the twins asked with impatient curiosity.

"Come now," Gibbons coaxed. He ignored the question and continued to press Temperance to step thru the door and break through the final barrier that kept her from her family. They could have no way of knowing what awaited in the hall. Still, she could tell that the air was ripe with anticipation. Even their best guesses would do little to prepare them for the truth of it.

She straightened her shoulders. For the first time she wished that she had managed something better to wear than the shapeless postulant dress that swallowed her frame. With her chin held high she smoothed her fingers over her hair and tucked one rogue curl into the tight chignon that sat at the nape of her neck. She had used to let the flowing locks fall freely down her back, accented with a braid or metal comb on occasion. Now, she must look more like a school marm, or the postulant that she had been, rather than their sister. She felt frosty and immobile. To remedy the bleak style, she set her features into what she hoped was a pleasant smile. Though the corners of her mouth shook with the effort, Gibbons' nod told her that she was as ready as she might ever be.

4

$\mathcal{T}$emperance slipped through the doorway on light steps that had been well trained to dampen any sound. Had the seven figures seated at the table not been turned her way, they might not have even noticed her arrival.

Her mother released a sound that was a mix between a gasp and a shriek. It was as if she did not know whether she believed her own eyes, that her daughter might once again be standing only a stone's throw away.

Isaac and Lucas shot from their chairs to stand with gaping mouths at their sister's arrival. Another gentleman, rose at their side. A very handsome gentleman Temperance noted. Temperance dragged her eyes from the stranger to look at her family. The young Viscount's mouth moved as if he wished to speak, but no sound came forth. The twins, known for their constant chatter and witty remarks, were unnaturally silent. Temperance noticed that the hands of Hope grasped the sleeve of her mirrored image in search of support from the shock that they had just received.

It was Mercy, ever the silent one, who first collected herself to speech.

"You're late," she said in an even tone. Her dark eyes assessed Temperance and found her wanting.

"E-Excuse me?" Temperance asked.

"We sat to tea more than ten minutes ago."

Seven sets of eyes that surrounded Mercy's petite form turned to look at her with dismay and confusion.

"Mercy," Temperance said gently, but Mercy would barely look at her.

"The pot will be cold," Mother said finally, "but I am sure Mr. Gibbons can have it refilled."

"Right away, M'lady," Gibbons said with a bow.

Temperance was unsure what to say to melt Mercy's cool exterior.

"We have missed you!" the twins cried. They still had the uncanny ability to speak in unison, Temperance noted. At least that had not changed. She smiled at Faith and Hope. Mother has once said, that she wished the next child to be named Charity, but the next child was her younger brother, Simon.

Her brothers stood, Isaac and Lucas. They were both taller than she remembered: their forms having lost the gangly limbs and sharp angles of boyhood. Temperance noted man who was not her brother. He was taller than both Isaac and Lucas and his dark eyes sparkled as his gaze lit upon her. Temperance lowered her gaze in confusion. Her father had entertained so rarely; that she had not expected her homecoming would be observed by a stranger.

The room erupted into conversation. Temperance found herself suddenly surrounded by her family. A hundred questions that could never be answered in such short succession passed their lips with Temperance doing her best to explain her arrival. What was said did not matter. In fact, afterward none of them would recall much about the conversation other than their elation at the return of the missing sister. It all went far better than expected. Not a tear was shed, for all avoided the topic that hung like a black cloud over the family: their father.

"Tempe, my dear," Isaac said, using the nickname he had used as a child and then corrected himself. "Temperance." He turned to her and then the unknown gentleman. "I present my sister, Miss Temperance Baggington. Temperance, this is my friend, Mr. Evan Crauford, son of the Viscount Pepperton."

Mr. Crauford bowed over her hand, and for a brief moment Temperance felt she could not breathe with the excitement of the introduction. His eyes bored into hers and she felt light as a feather. The conversation resumed around them, but she found she could not concentrate on her siblings. Her attention kept slipping back to handsome gentleman, Mr. Evan Crauford, her brother's friend. He must be a close friend, Temperance surmised since Isaac did not lead the conversation to the weather and niceties. Instead he shared happy family topics and Temperance noted with some dismay that Mr. Crauford was more in the know than she was.

Time passed and stories filled with laughter were shared as if she had just returned from a short vacation at the sea. She learned much of the progression of her siblings, at least that of her brothers. Isaac had taken the title and estate to his name, Lucas had nearly finished his education in pursuit of a position in law, and both Simon and Jesse, as third and fourth sons, had purchased commissions within the military and were currently off on a patrol near the coast.

"Thank heavens they had not been sent to the colonies or France," their mother said and the conversation would have moved deeper into the state of the war, although Isaac soon said that such was not fit conversation for the ladies.

Temperance did not have much to share. Life in the Abbey had been the same from the first day to the last, though she did fill her family in on what she could about her visits with Prudence and how she fared. It was not known that Prudence had run away from her abusive husband, and Temperance was not about to tell them that tale if they did not know. Certainly she would not speak of it in front of Mr. Crauford whom she did not know. It did not matter that he seemed nearly a member of the family; she would not be so loose with family secrets. If Prudence's flight became well circulated, she might not be permitted to keep the Earl of Fondleton's estate.

Only one servant, a pest named Perry, had known Prudence's tale, but he could not out the lady without revealing his involvement in his master's dastardly, and criminal, deeds. The man Perry had slipped off into the night, hopefully never to be seen or heard from again.

Temperance brought her attention back to the table. He brother was telling a story of one of the twins many escapades. She found her attention drawn to Mr. Crauford who was sitting in apparent rapt attention, a smile on his face. Temperance took the moment to study him. A smile seemed to be the natural expression of his face, just as Father's had been a frown. No. She would not think of her father. This was to be a happy homecoming. The others erupted into laughter while the twins tried to refute the tale.

"Do you have brothers and sisters, Mr. Crauford?" Temperance asked.

"A younger sister," he said, and a softness filled his eyes. "Teresa. I hope you will meet her in a few days."

"Yes," Isaac interrupted. "We are celebrating the renovations."

Temperance indeed felt that the air in the house was lighter than she recalled, as if some weight had been lifted at the moment of her father's passing. That, or the renovations that had been made by her brother, had brightened the rooms enough to feel like a different home entirely.

What had once been dark, burgundy walls were now crisp whites with threaded gold lines that sparkled in the distance. She complimented her brother's taste and declared it the most beautiful home she had ever seen.

"I would wager your standards are a far sight lower after living in an abbey," Faith laughed, "but we are all pleased with the progress."

"I thought a change was in order," Isaac admitted with a firm confidence that Temperance noted would make him a find lord. "Besides, the manor has not been used properly in years. It is high time we remedy that."

"I learned on my way here that the road is being repaired," Temperance said with a smile. "Is there more?" She sipped her tea and noted that Mr. Crauford's eyes were drawn to her, as hers were to him. She blushed and looked down, and then turned to her sister as she spoke, but Temperance felt the weight of his gaze nonetheless.

"Oh, loads more," Hope grinned. "The gardens have been re-paved for a stroll, and Isaac had roses planted. Those stuffy curtains have been removed from the dining room and it now boasts fine sheers and grandmother's candelabra, which we found, hidden away." She paused for a moment. "Best of all, we've exchanged rooms now that Isaac is the Viscount. Mother took grandmother's suite in the south wing and the rest of us all switched rooms and decorated to our own liking."

"Prudence's chambers have been left untouched," Faith continued picking up where her twin left off. "Or your own if you would prefer."

"None of us wanted to stay in our own," Mercy said casting a slight pall upon the conversation.

The room was silent for a long while as Temperance processed the information. Though it went unsaid, the new sleeping arrangements spoke volumes to the family's determination to forget its troubled past. She wondered how Isaac had been persuaded to agree to the arrangement on what could not have appeared as anything more than the whim of his sisters.

"My sister would have the whole manor painted pink

and filled with roses," Mr. Crauford confided with a jolly laugh.

"Surely not," Isaac said. "Pink?"

The gentleman chuckled at the choice of decoration.

"I should love to have the use of Prudence's rooms, if I may," Temperance whispered in time. She did not think a coat of paint could repair the memories of her own chambers, but she said she would prefer some shade of rose rather than pink. The gentlemen chuckled again, and Temperance felt a flush fill her face as Mr. Crauford commented a beautiful lady should always be surrounded by roses.

"Careful," Isaac commented, and Temperance wondered if Isaac would tell his friend that she was a nun, but Mr. Crauford toasted her with his teacup, and the company laughed. How long had it been since a gentleman commented on her beauty? How long had it been since she could accept such a complement? How long had it been since this house had seen laughter?

"Will you be staying long, Tempe?" Isaac asked rocking back on his chair. "We have not made the room over yet, but I can have it done in a month if I set my men to it. We've already ordered new linens for all the beds which are to arrive from London any day now."

"You've no need to rush on my account," she said with a grateful smile. "Prudence's room is fine as it stands. I promise is it much more lavish than I have become used to at the Abbey."

"How long *will* you be staying," the Dowager Viscountess asked with bated breath.

Temperance felt a flood of butterflies in her stomach

as she put her teacup in it saucer and looked into it as if she were reading tea leaves, but there was no telling the future. "As long as you'll have me," Temperance replied. She clamped her lower lip between her teeth as she looked upon the surprised stares of her siblings. Was she not welcome anymore? "I am not a nun," she added in hopes that it might clear up some of the confusion. She couldn't keep her eyes from straying to Mr. Crauford who was looking at her in appreciation. She felt her breath hitch and she tightened her hold on her teacup.

"What did you say?" her mother breathed.

Temperance dragged her eyes back to her mother. "I never took my vows," Temperance admitted with part shame, part relief. "I could not do it. The Mother Abbess said I must feel the calling in my heart, and I never..."

"Oh, bless the Lord!" Her mother shouted while she threw her hands into the air with joy. "My darling daughter has returned! I could not bear the thought of your most beautiful face locked away in a convent!"

Temperance grimaced and glanced at Mr. Crauford who noted, "Such beauty would indeed be wasted in a convent." Temperance blushed embarrassed by how personal this conversation had turned in front of what to her was still a stranger. How could he say such a thing when she was dressed in a shapeless sheath? She had always been uncomfortable with references to her beauty. Her mother had taken pride in it but Temperance had been leery that men saw little else in her. Still, Mr. Crauford seemed sincere.

"It is no wonder that Prudence always considered

herself lacking," Faith drawled teasingly. "How can one expect to follow in such glorified footsteps?"

"Oh be quiet and let a mother dote," the Dowager Lady Mortel swatted at her youngest child inadvertently shooing the twin that had not spoken, rather than that which had made the comment. Faith giggled while Hope glared at her. "You know you are all beautiful young misses, and I love you dearly, but I have not had the occasion to look upon this face for what seems an age. Though... Temperance... I must say...what is that thing that you are you wearing?"

"Clothed in sackcloth," Mercy said.

The entire table let loose with laughter, but Temperance was not sure Mercy meant to be funny. Sackcloth for penitence, and surely she did deserver to do penance for abandoning her younger sisters. Still, she looked down upon her shapeless grey dress and blushed hotly though she could offer nothing more than a shrug in response.

"Such lowly attire does not mar your beauty," Mr. Crauford commented, and Temperance found herself uncertain of his intentions. She did not trust men who extolled her beauty, and yet there was something trustworthy about him. She met his eyes and wondered what was it about the gentleman that made her want to trust him.

"Well," The Dowager Mortel said, "I believe your sisters have picked through your old things over time. Still, I believe we can manage to find something..."

"Not at all," Temperance replied. She meant it. There

was nothing from her past that she desired. A fresh start was exactly what she needed even if it was slow coming.

"I shall send a note to Mary Merton this afternoon," the matriarch said with a firm nod. "She should be able to fit you for a dress or two from her window, the rest shall be commissioned in time. Isaac, I think a ball gown is in order...considering."

Temperance watched as the faces that surrounded her broke into mischievous grins, all except for Mercy who seemed even quieter than she had once been. How did she know what was usual, Temperance asked herself. She had been gone for five years. She had no right to intrude.

"Please do not go to the trouble," she begged. "I did not return to be a bother." She had no need of fine gowns.

"Nonsense," her brother replied. Isaac was more than a year younger than Temperance herself but seemed to surpass her in age with his confident bearing. She wondered when he had grown so. In the last five years she reminded herself. In spite of herself, her eyes went to his friend, Mr. Crauford. Uncomfortable to once again find herself the center of attention, Temperance expressed her dismay, but Isaac interrupted her. "I shall not hear another word of it, Tempe. A new wardrobe shall be commissioned."

Temperance did not wish to be a financial burden to her family. Hadn't her father expressed how much the loss of her dowry cost him? Now, she could not expect her brother to furnish further income for his sister's care. She began to protest, but Isaac stopped her.

"The estate is doing well and shall improve in the

years to come," Isaac replied with a note of finality. "Do not fret about your dowry. Father did not put much aside for any of you, but my hope is to remedy that before the time comes that the dowries are needed."

Temperance felt self-conscious that Mr. Crauford might hear of these family troubles, and threw him a glance but he seemed unconcerned. Isaac also seemed not to care.

"I cannot promise to be able to replace yours entirely," Isaac said. "But I can at least offer you enough to meet your needs for the time being."

Temperance offered her brother her heartfelt thanks. She had no intention of marrying, and therefore had no need for her dowry. Still, the offer of a proper wardrobe was more than she had expected. Particularly because, as far as she was aware, her brothers thought nothing more of her leaving than an attempt to avoid an unwelcome marriage.

"Do you think Miss Merton can complete a suitable ball gown in a fortnight?" Hope asked with concern written upon her brow.

"The young woman is a miracle worker with a needle," Faith said. "I am sure she can."

"She has made several gowns for my sister," Mr. Crauford added. "In fact, Teresa has been pestering me to return to her."

"I love the dress she made for me," Hope said. "What about yours, Mercy."

"It is lovely," Mercy said dryly.

"A proper daily wardrobe I understand, but I have no need for a gown, I assure you," Temperance protested.

"Of course you do!" Faith replied.

"For what, exactly?" Temperance shook her head. "I have no intention of receiving invitations to any balls in the near future. I really would rather not socialize just yet, if it can be avoided."

"I'm not sure how you intend to avoid it," Lucas said into the periodical that he was browsing over his crossed knees. He held a scone in his hand and munched along as if unperturbed by the conversation around him. "What, with a ball about to occur in your own house."

"W-What?" Temperance stammered.

In her lifetime she had never seen a ball hosted at the Mortel Manor. She had heard tales of lavish parties long ago, but her father had never saw fit to host one.

"In a fortnight." The twins nodded in unison.

"I think it just the thing to announce myself to the Nettlefold community," Isaac said with a grin. "My sisters might have come up with the idea, but I heartily agree. It is high time our family returns to decent society. We have been, excuse my turn of phrase, *cloistered* for far too long." He winked at Temperance and she blushed.

"I cannot believe it," Temperance murmured.

"A lot of things are going to change around here now that I am the Viscount," Isaac continued. "Guests shall begin to arrive the day before the event. You have until then to make yourself settled, Tempe," Isaac said.

"House guests!" Temperance exclaimed. A ball where dancers might arrive in droves and leave the same evening was one thing. Guests, to take up the spare rooms for an extended stay, was quite another.

"I count myself lucky to be the first guest to arrive,"

Mr. Crauford said and Isaac poked him playfully. "I only hope that one of your lovely sisters shall save me a dance."

The girls tittered, but Temperance felt his eyes were just for her. She stared at a spot of the tablecloth. She felt entirely out of her depth. She had not danced for years!

"Please excuse me," Mercy said rising from the table. The gentleman stood as was expected. Mercy hastened away, and Temperance wondered what had upset her. Perhaps, Temperance thought her very presence had upset Mercy, but she did not know how to fix the rift that separated them. She turned back to Isaac.

"How many guests?" Temperance asked.

"The final count is not yet in" her brother replied. "But many shall stay for the month. Now that the manor nearly ready to be seen, I thought it just the thing." Isaac went on to explain that several of his longtime friends from Eton had hosted him for years without a return offer.

"We never faulted you for it," Mr. Crauford said, but Isaac objected. He now intended to make up for lost time by offering his hospitality. Many families already had made their plans for the season, but the winter months were ripe for the picking and several guests had welcomed the invitation for an extended visit.

Temperance felt as if she had stepped into a dream world. With the passing of her father it seemed that all the things that she had once hoped for her life were coming to fruition. She could not help but give in to the hope that blossomed in her heart. She was happy that no others in the house had succumbed to whatever aggressive illness had taken her father's life. Mrs. Hardcastle had mentioned that it had come on fast, and that the physician could find nothing to be done to remedy the sickness. Temperance could not help but think that all the evil in this world had been smote in one fell swoop. Things would truly be different now.

5

*A*fter the family had completed their meal, the gentlemen made their regretful excuses to go about their duties. The twins longed to stay and speak with their sister but had already promised a visit to Mrs. Lily Sharpton, wife to the young physician. The bright young woman had come from tenuous means herself, and the twins had bonded with her at once. Temperance was happy to hear that they might now venture into town and create such friendships. Excursions as such had been forbidden when she was their age.

Upon their departure, Temperance found alone in the tea room with her mother. It seemed her younger siblings had sensed Temperance's need to speak to their mother and had made themselves scarce. She was nervous and could see that the Dowager Viscountess was suffering the same affliction.

"Mother..." Temperance began.

"Darling…" her mother said at the same time.

They both laughed.

"I read your letters," Temperance admitted. "Just this evening past, but I wanted you to know that I had seen them."

"Come and sit with me," her mother urged leading her into the drawing room. Her mother rang for tea and then looked at her daughter.

"I supposed you had not read the letters at first," her mother admitted. "I cannot deny that I doubted that you ever would. I am glad for it. I meant every word. I felt so guilty. I was a horrible mother."

"No, you are not," Temperance said.

"I failed to protect my children. To protect you. I did not know what to do. I had not the courage, and…your father…"

Temperance placed her hand atop her mother's and offered a soft smile. "Let us not speak of him any further," she whispered. "There was naught that any of us could do at the time. Father was a powerful man. I am only sorry for the trouble I brought upon our family in my haste to leave."

"Temperance," her mother looked upon her with concern. "I hope you do not think that any of us hold you to blame for his wrath, or for your desire to escape it."

She did not think her mother was entirely correct. Surely Mercy blamed Temperance for abandoning her.

"We all would have escaped if we might have found the way. It did our hearts good to think that you were safe, outside of his reach. I wanted nothing more than for you to be happy."

Temperance bowed her head. How much she had longed to hear those words, she would never be able to express.

"Perhaps," the Dowager Lady Mortel suggested, "we might start anew. Let us put the past behind us and enjoy that which we have been given."

"I would like nothing more," Temperance agreed. "Only... there is one thing."

"I know what you shall say," her mother said with a resigned sigh. "You have returned but you would ask me not to parade you around the neighborhood for all to see. I would also wager that you are not receptive to my input on eligible gentlemen at this time?"

Was that so? Temperance wondered. Just yesterday she would have been sure, but now she considered Mr. Crauford. He seemed different than other men. Kinder perhaps. A part of her want to trust again, view the world without suspicion, but she was not sure she ever could. She was tainted. She could not be a proper wife.

"I do not know that I ever will be," Temperance admitted. "I cannot even consider it as of yet. Please, I beg you... do not think of me as your firstborn. Allow the others can court and marry as they would have if I had joined the convent. Let them not be restricted by my reluctance. I have no wish to marry. I had thought on becoming a governess."

The Dowager Viscountess took her daughter's request well. "As you wish," she replied. "I ought to have known as much from the beginning. I only wished to set you free of this cage long before you flew away."

"I understand, mother," Temperance smiled. She did understand.

"You always were stronger than me," her mother said softly.

"You did your best," Temperance assured her. Her mother, subject to her father's rule for the duration of their marriage, could do nothing to help her daughters save marry them off as quickly as possible. She had done what little she could within her means.

The mother and daughter linked arms and decided to take a stroll out in the newly paved gardens now that the rain has stopped. Nonetheless, it was quite cold. Temperance admired the smooth limestone path that had been puzzled together with an intricate pattern of broken shapes. It seemed strange that the broken pieces could make up something beautiful.

"Even after everything, I still missed this place," she admitted. "And I missed you all more than I can say, Mother."

"There is a beauty here," her mother mused. "A beauty that shall soon be restored, and stand as it should have been all along."

"Yes," Temperance nodded.

For an hour at least they walked from the garden to the lawns until the cooler evening air drove them inside. Their conversation was light, unhindered by the passage of time. Temperance felt sorry for her mother. Though she never mentioned it, Temperance realized that it must have been a terribly unhappy match for the aging woman. What joy did she have in her life? Her mother was not lacking in beauty, but she was no longer young in years and the bearing of nine children had taken a toll on her thin frame. She looked weary and drawn. After their stroll, the widow took her leave to rest in her chambers. A midday nap would refresh her from the excitement of the afternoon. She promised to come down to supper, but for now, Temperance was left to her own devices.

It was strange how familiar, and yet alien, the halls and rooms had become. She could walk each path with her eyes closed and yet found that even her memory of things that she had thought well imprinted had changed over time. She peered into each room, one after another, until she had inspected all of rooms on the main floor.

It was not until she cracked the door to the music room that she felt a wave of disappointment. Where her grandmother's pianoforte had once stood surrounded by an array of instruments and music stands, there was now nothing. Only a large empty rug, creased with depressions from the feet of the lost instruments. It looked forlorn. The harp that stood by the window had left its mark in the plush fabric but the object itself was no more. Not a single musical instrument remained.

The stark emptiness of the room had the appearance of one of her father's tempers. He would often be overcome with rage and make rash and permanent decisions. It was a shame, she thought, for it had once been a beautiful music hall. Saddened, she turned to leave the room and nearly ran headlong into Mr. Crauford.

"Oh," she cried stumbling backwards.

"I am sorry," he apologized. "I did not mean to startle you."

She stared at him, half in excitement and half in dismay. What was he doing here? She was acutely aware that she was suddenly alone with a man. No good could come of such an encounter, she thought, and would have moved past him to hurry toward a more populated part of the manor, but he spoke her own thoughts. "Such a sad room," he said. "It must be even more distressing to you."

How would he know such a thing? She wondered, as she paused in the doorway, but he answered her unspoken question.

"Isaac spoke often of his siblings, but none more so than you. I feel as if I know you, Miss Baggington. He said many nights he fell asleep listening to your playing. It soothed him."

Temperance did not know. How did she not know this of her own little brother?

"You must have been devastated when you learned your father destroyed the instruments."

"Destroyed?" she said shocked.

Mr. Crauford moved a bit closer and inquired, "Did you not know?"

She shook her head and automatically stepped back out of his reach. He did not follow. Her heart was beating a steady tattoo, but she was not sure her senses were heightened with fear. She seemed calmer than she ever was in a man's presence. "I assumed he sold them," she told Mr. Crauford. Money was of a premium with nine children. Father had often told her so but she did not repeat that fact aloud.

"No," Mr. Crauford said. "He destroyed them; smashed them in a fit of rage, the..." He sucked in a breath, and Temperance was sure the Mr. Crauford would have spoken unkindly of her father, but he held his tongue in deference to her femininity, though Temperance would have agreed with the epitaph.

"Isaac was livid," Mr. Crauford continued. "He said the man did it out of spite, as if to destroy the music in you."

The words stuck too close to heart. "I must go." She made to move past him, but Mr. Crauford's whispered words stopped her.

"I hope he did not."

"Did not what?" she asked.

"Destroy the music in you."

She was not sure what to say, but she no longer felt uncomfortable in his presence. Instead, her heart seemed to sing. He was different than Father and Lord Vardemere. She could see that now. He was gentler somehow. He had moved aside to allow her to escape, and simply because he did so, she no longer felt the need to run. "Will I meet your sister?" she asked. "At the ball perhaps?"

"Yes, I hope to bring her soon. Teresa will like you, I am sure. You can speak of Handel and Bach." He smiled and his face brightened like the sun. He had a wonderful smile, she thought. She found she wanted to make him smile.

Temperance nodded. It would be good to have a female friend. Prudence was married now, and the twins had each other and Mercy, what of Mercy? She wondered. "I will be glad to meet your sister." Temperance curtseyed as she stepped past him and he let her go. She turned back to him. "I look forward to seeing you again as well, Mr. Crauford," she said.

"I too am looking forward to the occasion," he said with a smart bow.

6

The following days were spent in a bustle of activity. Preparations for the ball, and the reparations of the grounds, were well in hand. Mary Merton made her visit to take measurements for Temperance's wardrobe. She was ecstatic for the commission and even more so for the knowledge that her old client had returned. With the promise of more balls come, the seamstress was glad for the work.

"I beg you to keep my return to your own knowledge," Temperance worried while she stood as still as a statue to avoid being pricked by Mary's pins. She was aware of how gossip could spread and did not want to be the talk of the town.

"Not a word," the young seamstress confirmed. "I swear to it."

Mary was easily excitable but Temperance had no doubt that she would keep her word. The young seamstress was a reliable and trustworthy asset to the community. In fact, Temperance was surprised to see the woman as yet still unwed. She asked as much.

"I shan't have the time for it," Mary scoffed. "What with the shop and all, I am too busy lately to spend my time seeking a husband."

"What of your sister, Phoebe," Temperance asked. "Does she not assist you? With the sewing I mean."

"My sister still helps as she can but she is often busy with her own husband and the smithy." Mary laughed and shook her head. "Phoebe has always been clumsy and I fear she never will grow out of it. She has a far better hand with the animals at the blacksmith shop than she ever had with a needle and I dare say she is happier for it. I suppose I shall have to put out a notice for a girl who can sew a fair seam before too long."

"Mrs. Hardcastle would know where to find your help," Temperance offered. The woman had often recommended reliable lady's maids and scullery girls for use at the manor.

Mary glanced at her with a knowing eye. Temperance wondered how much she knew about Mrs. Hardcastle's contributions to Temperance's escape. Not enough to make mention of it, Temperance determined, only perhaps only enough to have formulated a solid assumption.

"Yes, Mrs. Hardcastle does have the proper contacts," Mary admitted. "I might even offer a position to a girl from the school outside of town. I heard that they've fallen on a bit of trouble recently. I'm not one to speak of it but... terrible tales I hear." She shook her head.

"Have you many gowns to finish before the..." Temperance stopped herself. She was not sure if she ought to mention the ball. She did not know who her brother had invited, or if Miss Merton had seen an increase in work from the event.

"Yes, the ball!" Mary exclaimed without hesitation. "The entire neighborhood is abuzz with excitement. It has been at least three decades since anyone has received an invitation to an event at Mortel Manor and many have never seen it in their lifetimes. It shall be the highlight of the year!"

"The year?" Temperance laughed at the thought. She could not imagine that anyone would be so looking forward to a party with the Baggingtons. She did not say it aloud but her implication went unspoken. The Baggingtons had seen quite a demotion in their reputation in recent decades. Temperance doubted that there was anything other than gossip mongering curiosity that was stoking the fire of excitement.

"There can be no doubt." Mary nodded. "Most all the eligible gentlemen in the neighborhood are well paired and married. Save your brothers, that is." Mary's eyes grew wide and expressive. "And there are four of them."

"Only two shall be in attendance," Temperance corrected.

"Still," Mary shrugged and spoke through the pins that were held between her lips, "the ladies will be vying for their attentions from the start. Not to mention once it is discovered that you have returned!" Mary sighed clearly wishing she could be in attendance at the event.

"The *Ton* still whispers that there has never been so rare a beauty to grace our streets."

Temperance begged that she would not lead the conversation upon this path, but Miss Merton would not be dissuaded.

"Oh, we've had fine enough ladies here and there," the eldest of the Merton sister went on without pause as her fingers flew over the fabric. Before her very eyes, Temperance watched the draped fabric transform into an elegant day gown that fit every curve of her trim body like a glove. "...but when all realize that *you* have made your return, and are yet eligible, they shall fall all over themselves for it. I only wish I could see their faces when it is discovered." Mary made a cross over her heart with one finger and then touched her lips. "Still, not a word of your homecoming shall fall from my lips," she said. "This I promise."

Temperance took a deep breath. She was nervous enough about the ball, and the combined knowledge that her brother had invited visitors from afar. The last thing that she wanted was to be the center of a scene or an influx of gossip at the very sight of her. She had been isolated from society for far too long. Her ability to work the crowds or manage the appropriate, practiced responses was outside of her range of memory. I shall be a disaster, she thought.

"Mary, I cannot even recall the steps to a single dance." Temperance shook her head in shame. "I shall embarrass myself. There can be no doubt. I assure you, I shall be fodder enough to keep all of the gossips well-oiled for months to come." Perhaps it was best if she just remained in her room for the duration of the event.

She had mentioned the thought to Isaac on several occasions in the past few days, but he would not hear of it. He wanted to show her off, not for her beauty or availability to marriage, but in honor of her return and the completion of their family upon their entrance into a new beginning. Isaac stressed that the Baggington siblings were to present a united front as they stepped out anew into the Upper Nettlefold community. Prudence would be returning for the ball as would the Baron Halthaven. Although no formal announcement of their engagement had yet been made the baron's courtship of the young widow was well known. Simon, and Jesse would not be able to make the event, but the others would manage in their stead.

Temperance wished that she could make her entrance in some place that she might go unnoticed, like the overflowing streets of London. The truth was that Temperance had never had a formal London season. Her father had made his decision known and Temperance had put off her intended as long as possible with the knowledge that she would be married to a viper. When it could be prevented no more, she fled. In Upper Nettlefold, a society entrance should be all the more frightening. Everyone knew each other and it would not be long before all of the details of her life were presented upon a platter for all to discuss and make their opinions. The prospect gave her chills.

Temperance listened for what seemed like hours as Mary, who was remarkably well informed, filled her in on the goings on of the neighborhood. Tales of recent marriages, drama, catastrophes, and feuds seemed to plague every family in the region. Temperance had used to think that she had been cursed to have been born in such a place. Now, she was beginning to wonder if the world was simply ripe with far more turmoil than she had ever cared to admit. No matter the cause, she wished no part of it.

Mrs. Hardcastle had told her to find her own path. Temperance thought that a simple path, one that avoided such traumas and over excitement was more to her taste. She would easily forego a passionate love if it meant that she might have a steady and predictable future. As she thought of quiet and calm, the face of a certain Mr. Crauford appeared in her mind's eye.

She laughed at the thought. She had no interest in romance. It was only that, under the magic of Mary Merton's skilled fingers, she had given into the fantasy of the beauty that was being fashioned around her. She was very nearly a nun. She had no idea of how to continue in society, but her dress was a vision before her eyes. Mary Merton was every bit as skilled in her craft as her mother had been. Temperance could not help but long for the whoosh and sweep of a gown as she spun about a dance-floor. Not for her own pleasure, of course, but because it would be unjust to the elegant folds of Mary Merton's work if they were not shown at their best. That was the excuse Temperance allowed herself as she gaped at the creation that Mary had woven around her.

"Now, it is plain at the moment," Mary hastened to explain. "I'll trim it up right and perhaps add a bit more of a flounce. It is only a rough design all done in pins but it shall turn out nice enough."

"It is beautiful," Temperance breathed as she touched the fine material. "They all are. I shall be sure to tell all whose hands deserve the credit."

Mary's face beamed. With Temperance positioned to be the peak of the gossip in an already highly anticipated event, her donning of a Merton gown would do nothing but bring the small dress shop a horde of ladies scrambling for Mary's creations.

"Miss Baggington," Mary cooed. "Mama always said that if I could dress you I should never want for a thing. Even a rag looks like a queen's gown upon your shoulders."

"Say it is not so," Temperance objected. Mary had already admitted that she had repaired a gown for one Lady Charity Abernathy and, as such, the recommendations had been pouring in. She could barely keep up with the demand for her services, but she said she was glad for Temperance's patronage.

"I only want to say how honored I am that you should allow me to make your dresses," the seamstress said with a slight curtsy.

"No," Temperance grabbed the lady's hands like she never might have before having spent five humble years in the convent. "I am honored to be allowed to wear them."

The eldest Merton struggled to hold back her tears as she finished the appointment and rushed from the manor. This ball could be the final step in turning Miss Merton's small shop into a most successful enterprise.

Temperance hoped it was so. She had always admired Mary Merton. Temperance and her sisters as the daughters of a member of the peerage were expected to find husbands who would support and care for them. Miss Merton was a woman who made her own way in the world by the skill of her hands.

7

---

*A*fter Miss Merton's departure Temperance descended the stairs from her new chambers, those which had once belonged to Prudence, determined to seek out Mercy.

As expected, Mercy was to be found in the library. Somethings never changed, Temperance thought.

Floor to ceiling books in bound leather graced the shelves. Generation upon generation had collected the valuable items. Some were so worn that Temperance wondered if they had been in existence when man first began to make his recordings. Of course, that was not possible, but volumes filled with several indecipherable languages led to the mystery and aura of the library.

It was with a sigh of relief that she acknowledged that her father had not laid a temperamental finger to this room. The loss of the music hall was tragic enough; destruction of the library would have been unthinkable.

Temperance sat beside her sister, but Mercy did not even acknowledge her presence.

She floundered for the words to say. Finally, she blurted, "I'm sorry."

Mercy snapped her book shut. "You left me," she accused. "You left us all."

"I'm sorry," Temperance said again, but she knew the words were utterly inadequate. She put her hands over Mercy's and was surprised that her sister did not pull away. She only looked at her, and Temperance could see the hurt in her eyes.

"You had me and Prudence. I had no one."

"The twins..." Temperance began, but Mercy scoffed and shook her head. "

"I could not confide in them," she said. "They were innocent."

We were all innocent once, Temperance thought. "You sought to protect them," Temperance said.

"I did," she replied. Without another word Mercy stood, picked up one of her books and strode out of the library.

"At what cost," Temperance wondered. Was it possible that the twins escaped their father's predilection? Was it possible they were spared? She sighed. If such were true it was no thanks to her. Only Mercy.

Temperance sat for a long while at the table wondering what she could do to repair the rift between them. Nothing, she thought. Nothing could assuage the hurt Mercy felt. She had never felt so guilty as now. She simply sat staring out the window at the gray clouds. The

weather was a reflection of her own mood. Perhaps she
should have not come home.

TEMPERANCE WAS ON HER WAY BACK TO HER OWN ROOM,
when she noticed the twins slipping out the massive front
doors and across the lawn. Temperance hurried after
them hoping for some solace. Their lighthearted laughter
meant that they could only be up to their usual antics.
There was nothing more that she desired than to see her
sisters happy in their own home. As she looked at them,
she was sure they had been protected from their father. If
they knew of his perversions, they gave no sigh of it.

Temperance was gasping for breath when she finally
caught up to them upon the lane.

"Faith! Hope!" she called. The pair stopped and
turned with smiling eyes.

"Drat," Hope giggled. "You have caught us."

"Oh?" Temperance teased, "And what is it that I have
caught you on about?"

"Shall we tell?" Faith asked her twin.

"I am not certain..." the other of the pair replied.
"Ought we trust her with our secret?"

It was clear that they were teasing or they would
never have revealed so much already.

"Out with it," Temperance laughed. She planted her
hands upon her hips and gave them a stern glare. Even in
the convent she had never been well known for her
ability to be perceived as stern. She wondered if they
would listen to her, but Hope smiled.

"Come now," Hope prodded. "Take a guess."

"How might I guess?" Temperance asked. "I have not seen either of you in an age. I shan't have the foggiest what you are up to." She hung her head as she said so. The truth of the matter was that she no longer knew her siblings well enough to be certain of their activities or interests. It pained her that she was so out of touch with them.

"Temperance," Faith placed a consoling hand upon her sister's arm, "we are not so different as you believe. Trust your heart and your instincts. We are sisters always. You still know us."

Temperance was touched by their words, especially after Mercy's chilly reception. She searched her memories. Could it be possible that the twins were still about their same old haunts and games?

"You are off to the old storehouse?" Temperance guessed.

The twins nodded in unison with expectant faces.

"No!" Temperance exclaimed as the thought came to her. "Are you still imagining stories and acting them out for each other in the rafters?"

Hope laughed. "On occasion when we are feeling especially overcome with excitement."

"Now, we write our imaginings down!" Faith admitted.

"You have penned your tales?" Temperance gasped. "Oh please, might I read them?"

The twins had always seemed as if they lived in an imaginary world of their own creation. Temperance had long wished that she could turn her mind away from reality with the same ease. As children, their games and tales had kept all of the Baggington children entertained for hours. To think that they were still active in such sport, though in a more mature fashion, was surprising.

"Of course," Hope replied. "Though you must not tell a soul."

Temperance promised.

"Who else has read them?" she asked as they continued down the lane toward the dilapidated storehouse.

"None!" the pair exclaimed.

"Why-ever not?" Temperance asked. "Many should love to read your stories. I used to dream of them at night and wish that I could see them acted upon a real stage."

"We acted them for you!" Hope pouted.

"Of course," Temperance replied, "but I always imagined sitting amongst a crowd at some grand theater with a velvet curtain and a crystal chandelier."

"Well," Faith admitted sheepishly. "I cannot pretend that our imaginings are so far from yours."

"Have you sent them off for publication?" Temperance asked with a shocked gasp.

"Not as of yet," Faith admitted. "We cannot agree upon a man's name to use for the playwright."

"Though, that is our hope," Hope revealed with a grin. "Perhaps not for a grand theater, but if a printer would accept our plays we would be pleased beyond measure."

"I have no doubt that you shall succeed," Temperance said with a firm nod.

"If only we can muster the courage," Hope said in a

small voice. "We've yet to finish an entire play. I wonder if we ever will. It seems that I will go one way and Faith the other."

"But we shall finish," Faith said with confidence.

"I am certain of it," Temperance replied as they approached the storehouse in all of its broken glory. "You shall climb the mountain when you are ready and I have no doubt that you shall find victory upon its peak."

Such progress and feminine initiative was a bold statement for two females of only fifteen years, but Temperance was glad that their imaginings had kept many of the horrors at bay. She felt her heart swell with pride at the women that her sister's had become. Despite their lot, they had not been deterred in the least.

The pair seemed pleased with their sister's praise. With hesitant excitement they led her into the darkness of the musty old building. Up the broken ladder, missing a rung here and there, they climbed into the loft above.

There, Temperance gazed upon their workspace. It was rare for a lady to have access to a study or office of her own. Not that this could be considered as such. Still, the sisters had fashioned a space for themselves among the cobwebs.

"What is all this?" she asked with awe.

"Our brothers helped us arrange it the summer after you left," they admitted. "Father was away more often in his determination to bring you home so we were left to our own devices much of the time."

Temperance looked upon a double-long desk fashioned from a pair of wide planks that had been balanced upon two sewn logs. Temperance wondered how they ever got them up the ladder into the loft. The makeshift desk offered two crates for chairs and a hollowed knot in the wood to hold an inkwell. There, the twins could spend hours writing their tales and creating fantastical stories from nothing more than their own vibrant imaginations.

Off to the side, in the shadow of darkness, lay a thin mattress and a lamp of oil.

"What is that?" Temperance asked. She certainly hoped that her sisters were not up to anything untoward, hosting a private bed in their secluded space. She dared not accuse them of entertaining visitors, but could not deny that the thought crossed her mind.

"Do not get your bonnet in a bind," Hope said. "That is for Tuesdays... or, do you not recall our letters?"

The twins seemed quiet all at once as they looked upon their sister with expressions of sadness. Temperance remembered suddenly their letter that stated that they would wait for her rescue them on Tuesday nights from the safety of their private haunt.

"Oh my," Temperance murmured. "Have you been waiting all this time?" Her heart leapt to her throat and she knew the answer before she saw her sister's heads bob in acknowledgement.

"Every week, we waited," Hope murmured.

"Until father died," Faith continued. "Then, we no longer had need of it. Besides, it was clear that you would not come. Though, we never gave up hope."

Temperance closed her eyes, linked her arms around their necks, and pulled them against her.

"I am so sorry. I would have come, had I known

sooner," she cried. She explained, through her tears, that she had only just read the letters. She begged their forgiveness and swore that she had not meant to abandon them. To think of the small girls, spending their evenings in the musty storehouse awaiting, her return made Temperance's heart crumble to pieces at their feet. She could not express her dismay, but without hesitation the pair picked up her shattered soul and reformed it with the kindness of their words.

"We have never been angry at you," the twins explained, "only hopeful that we might find the same freedom."

She gathered the two of them into her arms. They had forgiven her, but Mercy had not. This she knew, and she did not know how to bridge the gap that existed between them, but this moment belonged to the twins. They shared tales of their wonderful nights spent in the loft imagining their rescue and the life that would ensue. If nothing else it had helped the creation of their tales. It had become a wonderful tradition and an adventure of which they could look forward to week after week. They had written several imaginative stories about the wonderful things ladies might accomplish if set free from the bonds of men. What a different world they had imagined, Temperance thought. What a wonderful thing it seemed.

Together the three sisters cried their fill and made their promises of love and commitment to spend the rest of their lives making up for lost time. Temperance had never felt so blessed, not even during her time at the convent. Here she stood, full of faults and flaws, to be received and loved by such kindhearted souls. Her reception had been almost too good to be true. Was her family so willing to forget that they might only focus on the good? It was a blessing, to be sure, but so very different from what she had anticipated. This, she thought as she spent the rest of the afternoon rediscovering the magnificent beings that were her sisters, was what family was meant to be. This, is what should have always been.

It was almost as if, upon his passing, their father had taken with him his evil. In this moment, there was only good.

Temperance bit her lip and determined that she must find Mercy and try to repair the rift between them. She too was her sister. Guilt laid heavily on Temperance's shoulders. She had known when she left that Father's eye would fall upon Mercy, but what she could she have done? Even if she had stayed, she would have been Lady Vardemere and taken away to his home; unable to protect her sisters. She could not even protect herself.

Again, she sent up a prayer of thanks for their family's deliverance. Though it was wrong to wish death upon any, she could not help but be happy that her father was no longer among them.

8
---

*P*reparations for the ball and the arrival of the gentlemen's twelve visitors grew more elaborate by the day. The manor had come to life as never before. Each beautiful architectural detail was brought into focus with elegant drapery, fine floral arrangements, and shimmering light that reflected off of the crystals that were hung from every inch of the ballroom ceiling. The carriage hall had been cleared and fresh straw scattered beneath the new watering troughs.

Inside the manor, the floors shone like mirrors and the hall was filled with the sweet scent of fresh flowers. Temperance could see her reflection as she moved about the room and tried to imagine a hundred or so dancers spinning about with their shadows trailing along behind them on the floor. The women would be dressed in their finest. The gentlemen would with silk jackets and crisp cravats. Perfumes would mix in the air and the scent would be heady like a dream. She felt like a child in anticipation of her very first dance although in Temperance's case it was not so far from the truth.

She had not even known that the estate had been in possession of so many silver platters and crystal wine glasses. Cupboards were opened and linens hung upon the lines until they brightened into a brilliant white from the sun. Like a small town in its own right, the estate bustled with excitement and purpose. The mood seemed lighter and the dark memories and ghosts of the past were expelled from the halls by the joyousness of the Baggington sisters.

Before she knew it, the eve of the event had arrived. Temperance woke with a flutter of anticipation that was foreign compared to the monotony of recent years. She knew that Mr. Crauford and his sister would arrive today. The thought brought butterflies to her stomach. Mary Merton was to make the delivery of Temperance's ball gown and despite her earlier protestations Temperance found that for once she wanted to be beautiful.

All of Isaacs's friends would be coming to the ball. The gentlemen from Eton would arrive with their sisters. Seven gentlemen and five ladies made up the party. When combined with a half-dozen Baggington siblings, the manor would be near to bursting at the seams. Most of the visitors would be arriving sometime around midday. Isaac had declared that everything must be completed before that time. As the Viscount Mortel, Isaac was thrilled to share his holdings with his dear friends.

"I could not have thought to bring them here while Father was alive," he admitted when they had sat down to break their fast that morning. "They would have been overcome with boredom for all that he would have allowed us. Worse yet if he had had a fit of temper in their presence..." Isaac shrugged and brushed a lock of hair from his forehead. For a moment Temperance remembered the boy he once was.

The late Viscount Mortel would not have hesitated to lay into his sons in front of their guests. In fact, he would have done so with pleasure in order to establish his role as the dominant male. Temperance could already see that Isaac would be very different from their father. For that, she loved him all the more. There seemed not a hint of their father's malice in him. If it should come out in time, Temperance could not say, but for now she could not help but respect the gentleman that he had somehow become despite his father's poor example. Perhaps Isaac learned from his friends' fathers about how to be a gentleman rather than from his own.

"You would not have been so unruly," Lucas teased his brother with a knowing grin. "Certainly not enough to ruffle the old coot's pristine feathers."

Temperance felt her mouth drop open but she quickly pressed it closed. She had never once heard her brothers make such an overt insult to their father.

"If there was a single thing that I accomplished that pleased our father, I do not know of it," Isaac replied with a shrug.

Temperance longed to hear more. The girls certainly shared their fill of woes between one another, but they had always made a point to keep their brothers free of that burden. Isaac, of course, was away at school for most of the time. Had the gentlemen a dislike for their patriarch as well? Perhaps for no other reason than his rigid ways and argumentative character?

Temperance musings were interrupted by the arrival of the musicians who came to place their set and conduct a short practice session before tomorrow's extravaganza.

"Temperance," Lucas smiled, "do you still play? You might join them for a song or two just for fun, as you had always wished to do."

Her brother was right. Temperance had once dreamed to play along with an orchestra or at some elegant gala with true musicians. She was impressed that he had recalled her long faded dream.

"Oh no," she laughed. "I have not read a page in these past five years."

"Not at all?" Hope gasped. "You played so well, and so many instruments. Surely it will come back to you."

Temperance shook her head. The Abbey had boasted a pianoforte and she had plunked out from memory a few hymns and carols at Christmastide, but that was all. Her memory flashed to the empty music hall that had been wiped free of its contents. She suspected that had been meant as a cut direct to her passion for the art, but she could not fault her father for being angry with her. She had no intention to return, but still, the twins may have enjoyed the music room, if they had been given the opportunity.

"I am afraid my fingers would not recall the notes," she smiled that Lucas still thought her proficient in the art. "Though, I should like nothing more than to listen, if it would be permitted."

The musicians allowed it. Of course they would never deny the request of a beautiful young miss, especially not when that miss was sister to the lord of the estate which paid their fee. So it was that Temperance followed the musicians into the ballroom. There, they settled in the corner closest to the outer doors. The cool air, once the doors were flung open would bring the players some relief from the heat that would soon accumulate with more than a hundred dancers in the room. It would also permit their musical tones to drift out upon the lawn and gardens so that any who wished to walk about in the cool air could still hear the music and the party within.

Temperance leaned against the frame of the door, her temple pressed to the wood and her eyes closed against the world around her. The musicians tested their instruments in a cacophony of scales that juxtaposed one another like knives scraping upon a plate. She gritted her teeth and waited for the inevitable; the moment when their souls would blend into the magical melody of all that was good and pure in this world.

A signal must have been given for the group began to blend, one after another, into the most ethereal of sounds. Temperance felt her heart sing with the music. She longed to give herself over to its simplicity, as she once had; to forget all and simply pour her feeling into the strings or keys, but still the music soothed her soul. Such music, for pure pleasure, was not permitted in the convent. Musical acclaim was to only be utilized in the honor of service, never for the advancement of one's own pride and skill. Temperance had loved the hymns but she soon grew bored with the droning sound of the nuns' voices in song. There was little variety and she could play the simple songs without thought or skill. She allowed her talent to fall by the wayside. Now, she wished she had not done so.

Her fingers moved of their own accord. She drummed the notes into the folds of her skirts and pretended that they were once again flying over the ivory keys.

She had been standing thus for an hour when the musicians declared themselves prepared and situated to their liking. She was loathe to see them take their leave, but reminded herself that they should return upon the morrow for a much greater, and more extensive, performance.

She turned away just in time to see Mr. Gibbons letting Mary Merton in through the door with a large box tucked under one arm.

Before she could control herself, Temperance clapped her hands together and pranced upon her toes over to the seamstress. She should not allow herself to become so excited over such a trivial thing as a dress, but it could not be helped. She had had so little to be excited about in the past, that she might allow herself the pleasure of a material gift from her brother. The gowns that Mary had made for Temperance's daily use were some of the most fantastic workmanship that she had ever seen. She could not even imagine the splendor Miss Merton would fashion for the ball gown.

The pair hastened up the staircase just as there was a knock upon the door. From the upper landing Temperance could see Gibbons open the door to a group of ladies and gentlemen. The guests had begun to arrive.

She was far too shy to wish to meet so many new faces at the moment, and even more shy if perchance the handsome Mr. Crauford was in attendance. Mary was a friendly and familiar face; besides she had an appointment. Temperance would not be missed. In fact, the others would not have even known of her arrival or perhaps even her existence. She doubted that Isaac had spoken of her return, intending to make his sister's reappearance a surprise.

"Oh Miss Baggington," Mary crooned over the box. "I dare say it is my finest work." Miss Merton looked abashed but could not subdue the hint of pride that threatened to break forth.

"Your work is always supreme," Temperance offered the compliment and meant every word.

"I fear went a little over my estimation..." Mary warned as she kept the box closed with her hands pressed firm upon it.

"You shall be reimbursed," Temperance assured the shopkeeper. She began to grow nervous. She did not care for showy items. She would already be a spectacle without some ostentatious design or frivolous extravagance.

The gown had been fitted with the underlayment set to Temperance's form. They had discussed a pale robin's egg blue that would be reminiscent of the summer but elegant enough for any upcoming winter events.

Miss Merton lifted the top of the box and peeled back the layer of tissue that had protected the crisp fabric during the ride from town.

Temperance could not contain the gasp that fell from her lips.

The gown was a vibrant blue, but that was where the similarity between the plan and the present diverged.

The gown appeared like a crystal blue liquid poured over pure gold. Never had she seen such a glimmering fabric. The trimming was simple, much to Temperance's relief. The design, understated. Yet, there could be no doubt that she would draw the eye of every figure in the room.

"It is beautiful," Temperance mouthed. She reached out to trail her fingers along the folds. The fabric was light weight and would fan out like a dream if she took a spin.

"Was I too bold?" Mary asked with fear.

"Oh, Miss Merton," Temperance cried. "I cannot think of the words to thank you. It is perfection."

"I know that you wanted to keep the design simple but when I received the sample of this fabric I just had to use it for your pleasure." The seamstress pulled the gown from the box and draped it over her arm so that Temperance might inspect if further. "See here," she pointed, "I've hidden a few buttons along the back so that you might add a cape come winter. A lavish velvet would be just the thing and no one would even recognize that you've worn it again."

"I shall wear this gown a thousand times over," Temperance replied. She cared not for the wasteful practice that was commonplace among ladies, especially those who could not afford such luxury, but wished to give the appearance of wealth. Many a gentleman had fallen prey to debtors in order to keep their wives and daughters in fashion. Temperance would never treat a man so. How was it that she even considered a man at all she wondered, pushing the thought away, but the face of Mister Crauford lingered in her mind making her flush with pleasure.

"I am glad to hear that you approve," Mary grinned. "Your hair is so dark, and your skin as fine as porcelain and with your blue eyes, I just knew it was made for you alone."

"You shall need to order more of such fine materials," Temperance instructed. "I am certain that you shall have at least a dozen such gowns on request once this has made its debut."

Mary Merton pressed her hands to her cheeks. "I shall not make another like it. That would be a disservice to you, Miss. Please do try it on," she said with a smile. "I have been waiting all week for this moment."

Temperance allowed herself to be dressed and laced into the magnificent ball gown. Both women stood in silence as they peered at her reflection in the looking glass.

"It is even better than I expected," Mary whispered after a time. "The blue brings out your eyes, just as I hoped, and is exquisite against your skin."

"You shall be called to London in no time," Temperance said with a shake of her dark hair. "Nettlefold is far too small a town for one of your talent."

"I should think not!" Miss Merton said with a resolute scowl. "My mother settled here and so have I. Ladies can travel for days to have a London gown made, longer for something French. They can certainly make their way to Nettlefold if they have need of my services. Besides, it would do the town good to have more visitors."

Temperance was glad to hear that Miss Merton had no intention of abandoning Upper Nettlefold as her mother had. The Merton family was prized for sewing abilities and Mary was the only seamstress that serviced the three nearby neighborhoods, with a little help from her younger sister.

"You should take it off before it wrinkles, Miss." Mary instructed. Temperance did as she was bid and watched the seamstress hang the gown. It looked like something that would sit on display in the window of a shop. Temperance could not help but stare at it, though she had yet to move to replace her own dress. When she finally felt a chill upon her skin she allowed Mary to help her back into the pale crème muslin. Since her hair had been mussed in the process, she tied it back with a ribbon and deemed herself fit for company. She would not put on airs, not even for the handsome Mr. Crauford.

9

*T*emperance slipped down the staircase after Miss Merton had excused herself. She could hear the tinkling of feminine laughter from the south parlor and so she made her way in that direction.

Behind her Temperance heard the sound of the front door opening and Mr. Gibbons' quiet acknowledgement. Temperance turned to see the twins race through the doorway and scamper to a stop at her side.

Hope was bent over at the waist in an attempt to catch her breath.

"Good!" Faith gasped, "We aren't late."

"We are late," Temperance did her best to contain her laughter at her ragtag siblings.

"Well, at least we are not last," Hope corrected.

Temperance could not help but shake her head. The twins had been off on one of their misadventures and must have forgotten that the guests had been set to arrive at midday.

"Have you met them, yet?" Hope asked as she craned her neck in an attempt to catch a glimpse from the hall. "Drat," she huffed. "I cannot see a thing."

"Well," Faith pressed. "Tell us all."

"I have nothing to tell," Temperance giggled. "I know no more than you."

"Lies," the twins replied in unison.

"I have just come from my final fitting with Miss Merton," she assured her sisters. "I have no more knowledge of our guests than you. Although I can hear several females amongst the crowd so that is to be celebrated."

Temperance hated to think the kind of chaos that would ensue if all twelve visitors were Isaac and Lucas' friends from Eton. Such masculinity might drive her back to the convent with her sisters in tow. The twins laughed and agreed when she expressed the sentiment.

"Let us venture forth as a trio of immovable strength," Faith said as she straightened her shoulders and set her chin at a proud angle. Temperance felt more like a bowl of Christmas pudding rather than a pillar of strength, but she followed her sisters into the south parlor just the same.

She was relieved that Faith and Hope's regal entrance, and the surprised looks that their mirrored images brought from the crowd, allowed Temperance to refrain from becoming the center of the focus. The trio was introduced all around and though she could tell from the appreciative glances of the gentlemen as they offered their nods, it was clear that they were all in awe of the rarity of identical twins.

A sharp glare from their brother set his friends to rights and they closed their mouths and offered simple compliments to Isaac's sisters.

Mercy was already well ensconced in the female group that had arrived and Temperance moved to make her introductions there.

She soon learned the names and relationships of the twelve individuals. Lady Katherine Dawson, a frail looking lady with pristine posture and one significant dimple on her chin had arrived with her brothers, David and Robert. David, Lord Dawes stood to inherit his father's Earldom while Robert had income enough to support a life of leisure and had no indication of a career at present. Mrs. Susan George was two years' wed to Mr. Edward George, the future Duke of Radamere and a distant cousin to the queen's nephew. There were two Thomases. The first was Mr. Leeson who was still at university. He was a younger son of a Viscount and self-proclaimed flirt, who was on the path to his apprenticeship as a surgeon at Cambridge. He had dark raven hair and vibrant green eyes that were unsettling to Temperance's taste. The other Thomas, last name Ridlington, was Lord Emery. His family had long held an estate along the coast and his father had been bestowed the title of baron. The new blood of aristocracy was still written upon his features but Temperance felt that he would settle to it if he married a woman who was familiar with the goings on of the peerage.

The last female, was Miss Teresa Crauford. She stood at the shoulder of her brother, Mr. Evan Crauford, only son of the Viscount Pepperton. Temperance found that she could barely take her eyes from Mr. Crauford. He appeared more handsome than when she had first seen him. Isaac was telling the company that the Crauford family was one of the oldest surviving families and the title had never diverted from a direct father-to-son inheritance. Such pressure to produce an heir must weigh heavily upon Mr. Crauford's shoulders, Temperance thought. Though, he doted well upon his sister and teased her often enough that she laughed and told him off for it. She seemed to cling to his arm for support. Teresa was the quietest of the women in attendance. Her discomfort in a crowd was already apparent. Temperance decided to befriend her at once in the hope of putting her at ease. She could relate to a shy inclination and she remembered that Mr. Crauford seemed to think that they would get along.

The last of the guests was Mr. Lawrence Fagean was the tallest of all in the room, including Temperance's own towering brothers. He was thin and gangly like a boy who had yet to grow into a man. He was prone to laughter and bumbling in his ways. In no time at all he was providing humorous entertainment for the entire group until they all ached with laughter.

Lucas and Isaac were already well known to all, having visited often throughout the years. So it was that the Baggington sisters, those four which were present, were soon peppered with questions about their interests and hobbies. At first the ladies were hesitant to answer but they soon learned to give just enough information to satisfy the question without revealing the whole truth. It was not as if they had anything to hide, any longer, but in their own way they were each protective of their secret pleasures. Too often once discovered they might be used against the ladies or taken away entirely.

"I hear tell that Miss Temperance Baggington has a talent with the pianoforte," Mr. Crauford said and Temperance blushed with the praise.

"Mr. Crauford has never heard me play," Temperance objected, but Mr. Crauford asserted that her brother professed her music was like the angels, and surely she would not call her brother a liar.

"I would not," Temperance agreed, and with much coaxing, she admitted that she had recently returned from Halthurst Abbey, but shared no more as to the reason or the tale. She only made a joke that she was not fit for silence and the Mother Abbess had begged her to please be on her way.

This news was met with a chuckle from the guests. Temperance was glad when the attention was diverted from her, to the twins, but noted that Mr. Crauford still watched her with an attentive eye. She found his perusal did not make her nervous; in fact, she felt almost protected by his watchful eye.

The twins said nothing of their writing. They made claims to long walks and visits to neighbors. Of course the latter had only recently become true but it gave an excuse for their frequent disappearances.

Mercy, once drawn out of her shell, was the only one that strayed anywhere near the truth. She expressed a pleasure for reading and drawing but claimed not to be overly skilled at either. Temperance knew that to be a gross injustice and said as much without hesitation.

Mercy, though modest, had a fine technique with a pencil and spent many hours tearing through books with ease. Mercy's cheeks grew pink with a blush and Temperance was pleased that her sister had allowed the moment of praise and attention.

The dining room had been set with a hearty luncheon to accommodate the surplus. When the party moved to sit to the meal, Temperance seated herself beside Miss Crauford, who still clung close to her brother though the gentlemen vied for his attention and did all that they might to divert him toward their conversation. It was not until he saw that his sister was well into conversation with Temperance that he turned his back and spoke with the gentlemen, leaving the females to their discussion.

"I never knew that your brothers had so many sisters," Teresa said with awe after the fingerling sandwiches were served. "I knew there were several, but I never had names and faces to put together. Why have you never visited?"

Temperance shrugged and admitted only that she had been away. She did not say that the Baggington women were not often allowed beyond their father's domain until Isaac became the Viscount.

"He spoke often of you all," Teresa declared. "Regularly referring to you as a whole so I could not guess much further as to your number."

"We are five in all," Temperance laughed. "Prudence should be arriving tomorrow for the ball."

"What a blessing," Teresa sighed. "In my family it is only Evan and I. Please don't misunderstand me," she whispered. "I love my brother but I have long wished for a sister."

"I have enough to spare," Temperance laughed. "I propose we share."

Teresa laughed and accepted the offer. Soon the twins leaned across the table and accepted Teresa to the family as well. She beamed and shifted her chair away from her brother, her loyalties altered for the length of the visit.

Before long the seats had been rearranged with the females at one end and the males at another. Temperance had never sat thus and enjoyed the conversation immensely. Mrs. George teased her husband without mercy and he shot her looks of mock betrayal from across the room. Every time that he thought the others were not looking, however, his features softened and the love that he had for his wife was written across his face.

Mr. Fagean and Lord Emery were soon discovered to be the most meddlesome of the Eton graduates. They led their friends through tales of their troublemaking days at school. Temperance could not help but listen in on the conversation. Never had she known that her brothers had gotten up to such dealings. It pleased her to hear of their happy tales. To learn that they had been allowed a raucous childhood amongst their friends did her heart well. She more than understood their desire to leave home as often as an invitation arrived.

It did not take long for Temperance to decide that she approved of her brother's guests. Each seemed decent and steadfast, though prone to fits of fun and laughter. Most of all, and she noted her sister's breaths of ease as they realized the same, not a single gentleman had made an untoward comment or motion toward the ladies: lighthearted flirtations and banter, perhaps, but never anything that might raise a brow.

The gentlemen were currently discussing a ride about the grounds.

"You shall leave the ladies to their rest, won't you?" Mrs. George complained. "I have been bounced about quite enough for one day. I would prefer to keep my feet on solid ground."

The other ladies seconded the opinion and it was soon decided that the party would divide by sex. The gentlemen bid their farewells and the ladies adjourned to the drawing room where they might take their leisure.

More than ever, Temperance began to look forward to the ball. If nothing else, she might spend her evening in conversation with Lady Katherine, Mrs. George, and Miss Crauford. That should provide all the entertainment that she required, she thought, but her traitorous desires brought to mind the handsome face of Mr. Crauford. Temperance determined that she would speak to Teresa of her brother, but the twins joined them, and the private moment was lost.

The twins declared that at tomorrow's event they intended to remain upon the dance-floor for the duration of the evening. As their first ball, they were determined not to miss a moment of the excitement. Mercy, declared the opposite. She would remain present for a small part the first half of the evening because her brother bid her dance with him, but she would then slip away early in the night to return to her solitude. Isaac was pleased that she had agreed to even that much for their mother had been trying for years to coax her out to social events about Nettlefold. Mercy had always refused unless she was permitted to make an early departure, but of course part of the problem was that it was her father's eyes which would settle upon her when she made an effort to attract a gentleman's eyes. Besides, she argued she was not friends with many from Nettlefold.

Temperance had initially intended to join Mercy in her plan to make a quick getaway from the crowd. Now, however, she decided that she would see what the evening brought and remain for as long, or as short, as she wished. The day began to draw to a close; the party reconvened and took an early supper, so that they might retire early in preparation for the following day's festivities. When the group began to disperse, Teresa turned to her new friend and begged Temperance to stay for the duration of the dancing. Though she was shy, there was nothing that Teresa enjoyed more than a ball. "I love to dance," she confessed.

Temperance's heart sank at the thought. She had forgotten one very important factor. She no longer recalled how to dance. The convent had no time for such frivolity. Temperance went to bed that evening worried about what sort of embarrassment the coming evening might bring. She worried over the dance she had hastily promised Mr. Crauford. Should she refuse and seem cold and standoffish or should she prove her incompetence? In the shadows of the room she could see the outline of the beautiful blue gown that Mary Merton had made for the occasion. She feared she could not do the garment justice.

After hours of staring at her ceiling with imagined scenes of her foolishness playing over and over in her mind, Temperance knew that something must be done. She crept from her room and through the darkened manor, wracking her brain for who might be able to assist her.

So it was Temperance found herself outside the guest chamber that held Miss Teresa Crauford. She knew her sisters would help but Prudence had not yet arrived, it was only the twins' first ball, and Mercy was not prone to dancing. Temperance considered her new friend, Teresa. She hoped the lady would not be cross for having been woken in the middle of the night. Still she felt that she could count on Teresa, even though they had just met, they had an instant rapport. Teresa was red eyed and confused when she cracked the door to peer out upon the face of her new friend.

"I need your help," Temperance admitted. In a rush she explained that she could not recall the steps to the dances that she had once known so well and fear of embarrassing herself had kept her from her rest. In five years she had forgotten and was now concerned that she would disgrace herself. "Can you perhaps speak to me the steps in the hopes that I might remember?"

Teresa laughed and slipped back into her room to pull a dressing robe over her nightgown. "Come, then. Let us go down to the ballroom."

"The ballroom?" Temperance repeated. She had not thought this adventure through.

Then, with a giggle, Teresa grabbed Temperance's hand and pulled her down the stairs back through the winding hallways and toward the ballroom. Upon slipper feet, the ladies snuck through the house. They did their best to muffle their giggles but when Teresa pointed out that Temperance had lost her nightcap somewhere during their race, the pair were forced to cover their mouths with their hands, stifling their giggles, lest they be caught out of bounds. Temperance had never done anything so shocking as to sneak out of her chambers at night and race about the manor. Her Father would not have allowed it. She could not have imagined the beating she would have taken if he had approached her room only to find her missing.

Perhaps Teresa had done such antics in her youth, but it was all new and exciting to the eldest Baggington. She only hoped that her cap might not be discovered and some false assumption made about her doings.

They slipped into the ballroom and proceeded to spend the next hour reviewing the steps to the most common dances that would allow Temperance to make the best of her evening. Teresa did her best to teach her new friend the waltz but with no success since neither of them could lead. Temperance had never learned it and Teresa kept forgetting the tune as she attempted to hum along and count the steps

"I am sorry," Teresa lamented. "I cannot recall the steps, but you have done quite well with the other dances. I am certain you will not embarrass yourself." She yawned and seemed truly disappointed that their excursion must come to an end.

Without prompt, Temperance threw her arms about Teresa's neck and thanked her with all her heart for the lessons. "You'll make a fine sister to someone someday," she whispered.

Teresa's smile beamed back at Temperance in the light of the moon that spilled through the paned windows as they walked back to their prospective bedrooms.

"I suppose that depends upon whom Evan marries." Teresa giggled. "Though I should choose you as my sister Miss Baggington if I were allowed any say in the matter."

Temperance felt her face flush hot at the implication. Teresa had spoken in jest. She could not know Temperance had been thinking on Mr. Crauford for some time now, but for her marriage was out of the question. Temperance shook her head to clear the thought and spoke to cover her embarrassment.

"It is a fair possibility," Temperance teased. "There are Miss Baggingtons in abundance." Together the women laughed and, in that moment, their friendship was set.

"We could be sisters, you know," Teresa said with a blush as they arrived back at her door. "If... well if I married..."

Like a mouse caught in the act of stealing cheese from the cupboard, she squeaked and covered her face with her hands. She whispered a rushed goodnight, thanked Temperance for their fun, and hurried behind the protection of her door.

Temperance stood and stared at the dark wood for several minutes before she turned to seek her own bed. Just like that she realized that the shy Teresa Crauford had romantic feelings for one of the Baggington brothers. Though, which one it might be, Temperance could not say, Isaac or Lucas, she supposed as the others were away in His Majesty's service.

Temperance pressed her lips together and did her best to contain her smile. She would not say a word on it, but she was determined to observe the fragile tendencies of her new friend. Temperance could not help but feel light and excited at the prospect of one of her brothers falling in love and getting married, especially to one so pure and kind as Teresa. Alone in the Abbey she had never expected to witness these moments in the lives of her siblings. Now, she was happy that she had returned home and could do so. She wondered which of her brothers it might be. She also hoped that whomever it was, he would be gentlemanly enough to not break the lady's heart. Love her, if they would, she thought. Or, let her down easy. Teresa seemed fragile and very willing to give her heart. Temperance walked back to her chambers in wonder. Teresa was the rare innocent that Temperance had prayed still existed.

She smiled and closed her door behind her. Perhaps all hope for love in this world was not lost. Her last recognizable thought before she gave in to the oblivion, was that it was good to be home. For all the pain that plagued her here, this was still her home.

10

The following morning dawned and Temperance awoke with a smile. She was actually looking forward to the day and the ball. She even felt that she might accept a dance or two, if only with Isaac or Lucas for a turnabout on the floor. Surely not from Mr. Crauford, the thought made her heart race.

Isaac had promised to open the ball with his eldest sister upon his arm. He thought it a lark to announce them both to the neighborhood at the same time. Temperance was hesitant about this plan but her brother seemed to think it amusing. At least, rather than hide from the crowds, he took pleasure in toying with them. The new Viscount would not be afraid of his peers. Temperance gave her brother the credit he deserved for his boldness and agreed to open the ball with him, so long as she chose one of the four sets that she felt she could perform with some proficiency. Besides, she thought, she did promise Mary Merton to show the gown at its best. What better opportunity than to open the ball with the lord of the house? Still, the prospect made Temperance nervous.

She glanced around the table. She did not see Mercy, who was usually an early riser. "Is Mercy well?" she asked.

"She and Lucas broke their fast earlier," Faith said. "She has already retired to the library."

Temperance nodded as she seated herself. She assumed Lucas was out for an early ride.

"Isaac said you agreed to dance the first dance with him," Faith said as Temperance placed her napkin on her lap.

"Your confidence is returning," Hope teased as she took a bit of fruit from the plate that morning.

"I would not be so certain," Temperance laughed. "I am still as nervous and bumbling as ever. Though, I am doing my best to not let it control me." She reached for the plate of scones and took one.

"Nonsense," Faith continued. "You laugh again. You hardly laughed at all when you first arrived."

"I concur," Hope interjected. "The mark of the Abbey is washing away in time. Soon, who knows what you shall do. You might even introduce yourself to a stranger!" She took a sip of tea, her eyes twinkling over the rim of the cup.

Temperance shivered with the thought. "I would never!" Temperance gasped. Even at her best she would never be so bold as to do such a thing. "And if either of you should do so, I will set Isaac to ordering you both a personal chaperone."

The twins shrugged as, Isaac and Mr. Crauford entered the morning room and greeted the ladies. The twins had had no problem as children slipping the watchful eyes of their governess. A chaperone would be no different. Temperance shook her head and laughed at her sisters. They were a pair to be reckoned with. She prayed for whatever gentlemen might take the twins as their wives. They would be in for a lifetime of trouble. Of that there could be no doubt. Hopefully, the gentlemen would have senses of humor.

"What trouble are you two into this early?" Isaac asked with mock sternness.

The twins just giggled.

"Have you seen my sister this morning?" Mr. Crauford asked looking directly at Temperance. She blushed thinking of how she kept Teresa from her sleep last night.

"Perhaps she is having a lie in," Temperance ventured.

"Ah, there she is. Good morning, Teresa," Mr. Crauford said, standing at his sister's entrance.

Teresa arrived late to the morning meal. She slipped into the room without returning her brother's inquisitive look, walked right past him, and took the empty seat that Temperance had saved at her side. Isaac seated her and Temperance noticed her high color. Was he the one? She wondered.

Mr. Crauford seemed highly pleased, as well as amused, at his sister's behavior. Once she had made her choice of seat he turned away and left her to her meal.

"Did you sleep well?" Temperance asked. She hoped

that she had not caused her friend to oversleep by having woken her in the dead of night.

Teresa's hand moved from the folds of her skirts beneath the table and dropped something soft in Temperance's lap. "Very well," she answered.

Temperance had forgotten entirely about her missing cap. Thankfully, her friend had retrieved it before any had noticed and raised questions.

Temperance had to cover her mouth with her napkin and turn her head to contain her laughter. All eyes turned to the guilty pair of ladies as they looked down into their plates and giggled. It was clear that all were waiting for an explanation, but neither Temperance nor Teresa were forthcoming. Rather, the pair set about their meal with singular focus. Though both of their brothers shook their heads, and Temperance's sisters pressed them for an explanation, they remained resolute.

When the attention and conversation had drifted away, Temperance reached down and tucked the cap into her pocket until she could return to her rooms. Isaac would have had a fit if he knew the ladies had been wandering about at night, especially with so many gentlemen in residence. Such behavior was unseemly. Still, Temperance had not had so much fun in as long as she could remember. She offered Teresa a wink and her friend returned the gesture in kind. The twins crossed their arms about their breast as they tried to catch the pair in the act of troublemaking. It was not often that anyone other than the two of them had been up to something.

The ring of the outside bell brought the attention of the others away from Temperance and Teresa.

"That must be Prudence," said the twins as they both jumped up from the table in a most unseemly way.

"I am sure that Gibbons will show her in," Mother said. "Please sit down girls."

The twins complied, but Temperance could see that they were only still with a mighty effort.

Prudence entered and hugs where exchanged all around, then the conversation turned to the Baron Halthurst, Prudence's suitor. Everyone was anxious for news.

"Hush," Prudence said sparing a glance to Evan and Teresa. "I am only newly widowed. The Baron is a friend truly."

"We are all family here," Isaac said, and then with a glance at Evan. "Well, close friends and family. There will be no gossip from this table, I assure you, Prudence."

Prudence still seemed rather closed lipped about the Baron Halthurst, but the twins promised to get all the news from Prudence before the night's end.

THE LADIES RETIRED TO THEIR DRESSING LONG BEFORE THE ball was set to begin. Temperance had forgotten how much effort went in to the feminine preparations for such an event. Wearing a simple sheath as a novice had taken no time at all. She did not want to appear vain, but she did want to look nice for the event....for Mr. Crauford, she told herself and then pushed the thought away. There could be nothing between them. She was being silly. She would be a spinster; perhaps a governess, but never a wife. She volunteered to set Mercy's hair and hoped it would bring back the camaraderie they had as children.

She remembered long nights when she brushed Mercy's hair to soothe her and perhaps herself. They had sat in companionable silence then now it seemed strained.

She concentrated on setting Mercy's hair into curls. Mercy had been singularly closed mouthed, not even commenting on the hairstyle, but when Temperance had finished dressing Mercy's hair, her sister seemed to lose a bit of her stoic demeanor and offered to comb Temperance hair in turn. Mercy piled Temperance's hair upon her head in a soft pattern that was much more appealing than the harsh bun that she had been used to wearing.

"Thank you," she said sincerely.

Mercy answered with a taciturn "Your welcome."

Temperance looked at Mercy's handiwork in the mirror. A string of crystal beads was woven between the curls so that it might catch the reflections of light as she moved about the room. Temperance was amazed. When had her little sister become so adept? There were so many things she did not know about her siblings, and she wanted to. She wanted to be part of the family again.

Although the twins offered several possibilities, Temperance refused any additional jewelry. The gown itself was a work of art and she did not wish to take away from the detail that had been worked into the fabric itself.

They sampled some cheese and biscuits before donning their gowns. None of the ladies wished to ingest a full meal before lacing themselves into their elaborate dresses. Hope reminded Temperance to sip her glass with caution so that she might not fall prey to the need for relief. It all seemed very complex to Temperance, who had long been outside of the realm of social interactions.

"You may hold a cup, if you wish," Faith explained, "but only if you must deny an offer to dance."

"If you care to be asked, set your cup aside and free your hands," Hope said with a nod. "Gentlemen are more like to request the attentions of a lady they feel is otherwise unengaged."

"If a gentleman pays you a compliment do not grow cross as you have a tendency to do," Prudence scolded, though it was clear that the sisters were enjoying the view of Temperance attempting to catalog their knowledge. "Offer a nod and a word of thanks, but no more. You don't want to encourage too much or you shall be named a flirt."

"Baggage," Prudence teased.

Temperance grinned at her. It did her heart good to see Prudence so happy. She deserved happiness, Temperance thought.

The twins continued to bombard her with advise. Much of which she thought was only to tease her. They thought it a lark that the youngest should give instruction to the eldest.

Still, Temperance's head spun with remembering the do's and do not's of proper etiquette. What had once come so naturally now seemed an effort. It was almost as if every interaction was an intricate dance in itself and she was terrified that she might misstep over the course of the evening.

"Do not fret so," Hope laughed. "Stay near those that you know and we shall guide your hand. If nothing else claim an ache to your head and slip away for a time. That is the one benefit of a ball in your own home."

"I am not ready for such excess. I have been a simple sister for too long," Temperance said with wide, fearful eyes. "I fear I might slip away for the entirety!"

"You had best not!" the twins exclaimed. "There are few enjoyments as pleasurable as a ball. You would regret it."

Mercy clucked her tongue as if she were not inclined to agree to the twins' assessment. However, she too would spend some of the evening with the crowd, though she had made it clear that she had every intention of slipping away once she had been seen. She told Isaac that she was only appearing for his sake, but did not intend on staying for the entire ball.

Temperance smiled at the image of the five Baggingtons in the looking glass. Dark hair and dark eyes, all. They were nothing like the fair haired beauties that covered the streets of Nettlefold. Prudence had often said that their coloring made them look plain, but Temperance swore that it had the opposite effect. Their features made them stand out amongst the crowd. Certainly they were identifiable as sisters if nothing else.

11

---

*T*emperance and her sisters made their way to the main floor where they would greet the arriving guests at the entrance to the ballroom. Their visitors milled about the room as they waited for it to fill. A smile and a wave to Miss Crauford, Lady Katherine, and Mrs. George had the females abandoning their gentlemen to greet the Baggington sisters. Compliments were passed back and forth. The twins promised to make introductions for the other ladies to the locals attending. Temperance could not offer so much as she had fallen out of touch with every resident of Nettlefold, including her own family. She too would need to be reintroduced.

"Are there any eligible gentlemen that I should keep an eye open for?" Teresa asked with a sly grin.

The twins shrugged and began a lazy list of several local bachelors. Most of those of note had recently been wed or sworn themselves to bachelorhood.

"I had thought your sights already set," Temperance leaned in to whisper to her friend alone.

Teresa feigned no recollection of the confession, though her nervous laughter revealed that she knew exactly what Temperance had referenced.

"Which of my brothers has struck your fancy?" Temperance pressed. She linked her hand through her friend's and turned their bodies so that they might make a conspiratorial stroll about the room. Some guests had arrived and were milling about, but there were still a few minutes yet before the throng was set to arrive.

"You would like to know my secret?" Teresa laughed. "No, you must guess."

"Isaac is eldest and well titled," Temperance mused but Teresa's face remained resolute. "No? Have you an interest in law? Lucas is set upon that track."

"Surely he won't actually practice law," Teresa said.

"He is the second son," Temperance said. "He will make his own way."

Teresa wrinkled her nose.

"Or perhaps you prefer the look of a redcoat on Simon, or Jesse, which to choose…"

Teresa giggled but revealed nothing. There was too much fun in the game and it gave them something to talk about.

"What of you?" Teresa asked. "You are not married."

"Heavens, no," Temperance scoffed. "Nor do I wish to be."

"Not at all?" Teresa said with real shock. "I have dreamed of it my whole life."

"Not I," Temperance admitted. "If a lady could make

her own way, I would certainly do so. It is freedom I desire not censure." Even as she spoke the words, she thought of Teresa's brother. How much of her freedom would she give up for Mr. Crauford? No. She reminded herself, men were brutes, no matter how nice they might appear. "I have no need, or want, for a man to dictate my every thought and action."

"Why would a gentleman do such a thing?" Teresa scrunched her nose as if the thought made her smell something foul.

"I forget that you possess an idyllic world view," Temperance laughed. "I shall not crush your fairy story perspective. I shall only say that I am not so confident in men and the world of romance as you are, my friend."

"Then I shall endeavor to change your view," Teresa laughed. "There is much good to be found. How can you have such a poor opinion of men with four fine brothers?" Miss Crauford had been sure not to give away her preference and Temperance applauded the lady's ability to tease.

"You were fortunate enough then to meet *only* my brothers," Temperance replied with a forced laugh. "I assure you, there are monsters afoot in Nettlefold. You must watch your step." She said as much in her best attempt at a haunted voice. Teresa enjoyed the game and they turned at once to tell tales of frightening creatures that roam about the darkened forests at night. Temperance let a thin smile escape her lips, as she thought of darker things, but she did not crush Teresa's fancy.

By the time they made their loop, Temperance was

forced to join her mother and siblings in their reception. She left Miss Crauford upon the arm of her brother, who stood amidst the rest of the men of their party.

"You shall save a dance for me, will you not Miss Baggington?" Mr. Thomas Leeson interrupted with his well-practiced grin. Temperance could see that he was not used to being denied but felt no threat from his person here in the crowded ball room, so she accepted.

"I would ask for a dance as well, Miss Baggington. If you would be so kind?" the other Thomas begged before she could be off.

"Of course," she said with a nod. Lord Emery beamed with delight. Despite his reserved demeanor, she could sense that he would very soon find himself a lady upon which to devote his attentions. He, she thought, would be the next to marry of the set for there was something about a gentleman's manner that changed when he had decided to take a wife. Lord Emery had a seriousness about him, unlike his counterpart, who was in search of a muse for the evening and nothing more.

She bid both gentlemen a temporary farewell and rejoined her sisters.

"Mother?" she said after a while, having not actually recognized her own parent in that moment. Her mother wore a dress of pale gray with purple piping. Her hair was in a fashionable updo. Temperance had never seen her so. She always wore a haunted look, but now that was gone. "You look... different."

"A widow cannot wear black her whole life," the Dowager Mortel declared. "I felt the need for a little color, this evening. Black never did suit my taste. Half mourning is better."

Temperance did her best to keep her jaw from dropping. She had not expected her mother to mourn for long. It was not as if the Dowager Viscountess had had a happy marriage. Still, the idea that her mother might find herself another husband, in time, was fascinating to Temperance. Her mother's life had always been devoted to her children, with nothing left to herself. Temperance wished that some fine widower or such might make her mother laugh as she never had before. The sad lady deserved some happiness after all the years imprisoned beneath her husband's rule.

"Well," Temperance pressed a kiss to her mother's cheek. "You look beautiful. I do hope you enjoy the ball."

"Oh no," her mother replied. "I shall retire early, as is expected. It was only that I do not wish to speak of sorrow all night long."

"Nor do I, Mother," Prudence agreed, although she was still in black. "If I had known you had gone to half mourning, I would have done the same."

Temperance pressed her lips together and said no more. There were none of the Baggingtons who wished to broach *that* topic on such a beautiful night. Perhaps their mother had been right to make the statement with her dress. The Baggingtons were done speaking of their late patriarch. Tonight, they would celebrate the new Viscount and forget the old once and for all.

She laced her fingers into her mother's hand and offered a conspiratorial squeeze. When the doors opened, they were ready.

Temperance greeted guests for the first half hour with her siblings before she could take no more. The room was filled to bursting and there were still many more to come. She could hardly recall any of the names of the wives and friends that had come to Nettlefold since she had last made her rounds. Only those that had always held property, such as those of Fotherington Park, Nettlefold Chase, Westwood Hall, Hallingbrook Grange, or Torsford Abbey were able to spark her memory. Still, what had once been sons and daughters were now lords and ladies. Much had changed in just a few short years.

"Come now, we must open before the crowd takes up pitchforks and demands our heads!" Isaac teased as he appeared beside her. "I cannot greet another person else I shall lose my voice to a whisper."

"This ball was your idea, Isaac," she laughed. "Regretful so soon?"

"Not at all sister," he replied. He offered his arm, which she accepted. He led her to the center of the floor. The room remained clear until the Viscount nodded his permission to the players. Then, he swept his sister across the floor; her shimmering blue gown drawing gasps and sighs from the crowd. Feminine eyes would have glared darts had the news that she was his sister not circulated from the first note. Their hungry eyes gazed upon the eligible young lord and the sister woman who was no threat to their plans. After the first round, other dancers stepped forward with their partners and joined in the set. Temperance could not help but be surprised at how quickly the massive floor filled. She did not recall so many people living along the borders of the winding

Nettlerush River. It seemed that the neighborhood had exploded in numbers. Or, perhaps, she thought, the Baggingtons had simply been too isolated to notice.

Her brother teased her, as brothers are meant to do, for a misstep here and there. Still, he offered his strength so that he might guide her along and mask her blunders. Even if he made the false claim that she had stood on his foot, which she refuted with vigor. As it was, Temperance quite enjoyed her first dance though she was not convinced that she would be willing to chance a second with a stranger, despite her earlier agreements.

Before she could make her resolution, Mr. Leeson appeared to stake his claim for the second set. Isaac handed her over to his friend and moved to claim another of his sisters for the next. He had promised each their turn and would satisfy that duty before moving on to the pleasure of his female guests.

Mr. Leeson peppered her with tales of her brother's misadventures. He was quick to laugh and had a reserve of jokes that had Temperance's sides aching before the song was over. She thanked him for the honor and agreed to introduce him to an old acquaintance, Lady Isabell Rutherford, who had caught his eye with her elegant velvet gown in a rare deep purple, but it was known that beautiful lady was already spoken for, and she told him so.

"Not so until his ring is on her finger," he joked.

Temperance made the introduction and was soon left to stand alone as the pair moved to the floor. She decided to search out Miss Crauford and ensure that she was enjoying the evening. Teresa was found with Mr. and

Mrs. George. Their backs were turned and they were in conversation with another guest. Temperance slipped into the group and felt her breath catch at once as a wide, victorious grin stared back at her. Lord Vardemere. She could not breathe.

"Miss Baggington," the cool voice said with ease. "I was just getting to know your new friends."

"Lord Vardemere," she said with as much confidence as she could muster. She was sure her voice shook from pure terror. She had no idea how he had secured an invitation to the ball, but she was certain that her brother and mother had no knowledge of it.

"Lord Vardemere was just telling us how you used to know one another," Teresa said with a smile. It was clear that Lord Vardemere had charmed them into thinking that he was a close family acquaintance. Temperance was stuck dumb with the thought. She had no idea how to refute the relationship.

Temperance thought she might be sick as Lord Vardemere continued in his oily voice. "Yes, actually Miss Baggington and I were engaged at one point, if you would believe such a thing," Lord Vardemere delivered the news with such ease as to hide all hint of offense. "A terribly broken heart I had," he lied. "That was, of course, before she decided on a life of the cloth. I see now that it was not entirely true."

The others looked shocked at the revelation. Three pairs of eyes watched in horror, unable to comprehend how to extricate themselves from the difficult conversation that they had just entered. Mr. and Mrs. George excused themselves with covert looks of apology to Temperance. They slipped away to the dance floor, but remained near enough in case the ladies were in need of them. Lord Vardemere was far too practiced to make a scene. He preferred to toy with his prey, and was taking great pleasure in Temperance's discomfort.

"How fortunate for you," Temperance replied with no attempt at civility, "to have found another woman who was to satisfy your need of a wife. I meant to offer my congratulations, Lord Vardemere, upon your nuptials. I was sorry to have missed the happy event." Her voice dripped sarcasm.

"She is young, skinny and not well suited for childbirth," Lord Vardemere said with a shrug. "I am pained to say that she is bound to the home in this difficult time. I have my doubts that she will survive the arrival of my heir." He had the smallest bit of decency to attempt appear morose, but Temperance could tell that it was insincere.

Temperance felt as if she might faint. Her hands began to shake and she wanted nothing more than to race away to the safety of her room and not return until every guest had gone. She sent a heartfelt prayer heavenward for the young Lady Vardemere's safety; both in childbirth and from her husband. If the lady did succumb to death, Temperance was certain Lord Vardemere would not be upset in the least. She wondered if the leech would attempt dispose of her once she was unable to keep him satisfied. Or, worse yet, now that he had been made aware of Temperance's return. She could not bear the thought of causing another woman pain. The hunger in Lord Vardemere's eyes gave her chills and she could see that he would not be put off a second time. She linked her arm into Teresa's and made a muffled excuse to leave. Before the ladies could turn full away, Lord Vardemere interjected.

"Ah but I was hoping for a dance," he crooned. "Miss Crauford... If I may."

The lowest of all blows, Temperance thought, that she might have to turn her friend over to his venomous hands. Temperance shook with fury. Teresa's finger's bit into Temperance's arm and she knew that the lady wanted nothing to do with the offer. Still, it would be impolite to turn it down after having just made his acquaintance.

"Actually, Lord Vardemere," Temperance said with as much courage as she could muster, "the Cotillion is my favorite dance."

"Strange," he replied with a knowing grin. "I had always thought you preferred the Boulanger."

"Not at all," she lied. "If Miss Crauford would not mind, I would much rather offer my own company."

Teresa shook her head. She would not wish to leave her friend to the fiend; still she shuddered to partner him herself. Temperance gave her new friend's hand a squeeze and accepted Lord Vardemere's arm. He had played his hand just as expected and she had leapt to her friend's defense. He always had been skilled at maneuvering his way.

"Always the martyr," he whispered into her ear as they joined the others upon the floor. Temperance did her best not to visibly cringe. "You should have remained at the convent, cold as you are."

She turned her head away, and resolved not to say a word no matter how he poked or prodded.

"You know none shall have you now without a dowry," he hissed. "Why, I have already been paid so I might as well complete the purchase. I could be convinced to overlook your behavior, if you begged."

She turned her head even further. She refused to look at him. She certainly would not beg for anything from him. Tears welled in her eyes and she opened her eyes wide to keep them from falling. She hated every inch of their bodies that came in contact. It was as if he would forever leave burns where his hands rested. She wished that she might shake them off, but he was *Ton*, regardless to how loathsome he was.

"Come now," he pulled her further against him and took a long sniff of her hair. "You should be honored that I would even consider you now." His pleasurable sigh made her ill, and she tried to pull away but he held firm.

"I would hate to think what your *wife* might say of such statements," she spat, unable to remain silent when it was clear he would not be dissuaded.

"She is nothing," he scoffed. "A mere inconvenience. Hardly worth looking at when compared to... this."

His eyes roamed over her body, enhanced by the beauty of the gown, and it was if she could feel his gaze upon her skin.

"What a shame that your father passed," he crooned. "He would have made good on our deal."

"I am sure he would have," Temperance said between clenched teeth. "The wretch."

"Now Miss Temperance, it does not do to speak ill of

the dead," Lord Vardemere seemed not at all bothered by the loss of his friend. In fact, he seemed rather amused at Temperance's fervent response. "He always spoke so highly of you. Besides... more for me." He sniffed her hair again, nearly drooling upon her.

Once again she attempted to wrench herself away. This time, she did not care if she drew the look of the entire crowd. Still, for all his additional years, Lord Vardemere was not lacking in strength. His grip tightened.

"Unhand me," she growled.

"You have always been too proper to make a scene," he replied. "Your father did well to ensure that his daughters were compliant."

She was just about to push against him, scene or not be damned, when a voice at her side called her name.

"Miss Baggington!" Mr. Crauford said with a friendly grin. "I've been searching the floor over. You did promise me the next set."

He turned to Lord Vardemere who was clearly annoyed at the arrival of the young gentleman, but the elder was quick to feign a friendly nature in return.

"Do excuse us," Mr. Crauford continued with a ready smile upon his face. "I hate to interrupt but Miss Temperance assured me that her card was filled for the rest of the evening so I have come to collect upon her promise lest I be forgotten entirely."

Mr. Crauford had such a friendly face and good natured grin that Lord Vardemere could do nothing but hand the lady over. With a flick of his coat tails he turned on his heel and stormed from the room. Good riddance, Temperance thought.

Temperance could barely form a thought as Mr. Crauford took his place and led her about the floor, twirling as she took the steps in his arms she felt at once in a dream. She took a series of deep breaths to control her trembling as relief paired with excitement washed over her entire body. Once she had collected herself she tilted her head and stared at Mr. Crauford with a puzzled expression. He was smiling at her, his eyes sparkling with good cheer. They were both well aware that she had never agreed to a dance, nor was she set with partners for the rest of the evening. "Thank you," she murmured.

"Teresa found me in a panic and demanded that you be set free," he said with a shrug. "She seemed to think you had been coaxed onto the floor in her defense and even had a few choice names for the gentleman in question."

"No one should have to dance with Lord Vardemere," Temperance said with more venom than she intended. She grimaced and tripped and Mr. Crauford pulled her close masking her awkward step. She attempted to apologize, but Mr. Crauford would not have it.

"My sister is not prone to exaggeration or dislike," he explained. "If she declared that there was concern, I should believe it in an instant. Even now I believe she has gone in search of Issac and Lucas to have Vardemere removed."

Now, more than ever, Temperance understood Teresa's unique perspective. With a protector such as her brother, she had little to fear from the world of men. He had managed the subterfuge with ease and grace. He had left no cause for a scene or hard feelings between the gentlemen. He had simply stepped in and managed the situation so as to extricate his sister's friend without hesitation and Temperance was more than grateful.

"Thank you," she said after a long moment of silence. "I shall be in debt to both you and your sister for your good deed."

Mr. Crauford shrugged and seemed unwilling to accept her thanks. Instead, he turned to her with a genuine smile.

"Payment enough would be to not let the moment mar your evening," he offered. "My sister takes great pleasure in a ball. I should not wish to see her enjoyment, or your own, lessened by one so base."

Temperance nodded and shifted herself more comfortably in his arms so that she might give herself over to the dance. She hardly remembered the steps practiced the evening prior, but Mr. Crauford led her along well enough that after a few rounds she began to feel at ease. With his strong arms around her, she felt comfortable and protected.

By the time the music drifted to an end she had nearly forgotten about the encounter that had led them to partner one another at the first. Not, she amended, that she would ever truly forget Lord Vardemere's intrusion. It was only that, Mr. Crauford had been right. She should not allow her evening to be spoiled by one so undeserving.

Temperance thanked the gentleman for the dance, the rescue, and for soothing her nerves. He bowed kissing her gloved hand and his lips a light caress over her knuckles. His kind eyes were filled with promise and a flutter blossomed her chest. What did this mean? She had resolved to harbor no feeling for the male sex, but her heart seemed to think otherwise. She paused a moment, looking into his intense dark eyes. Then, she rushed off to find his sister and thank her for being a true friend. She turned back at the last moment to see Mr. Crauford watching her. A flush ran through her, but she did not meet his eye.

THE REST OF THE EVENING WENT OFF WITHOUT INCIDENT. Temperance did her best to observe Miss Crauford's pattern of behavior to determine which of her brothers her friend had developed an interest in, but saw nothing that gave cause for confirmation. Teresa danced with both Isaac and Lucas once apiece: Temperance, the same. Temperance attempted covert questioning of her brothers, but they too revealed nothing of interest more than a fondness for Miss Crauford and her brother. Teresa was neither flirtatious, nor fawning, over either of the Baggington sons that were in attendance. Temperance began to wonder if it might be Simon or Jesse, who were not present, who had caught her friend's eye.

All of the notable families of Nettlefold, near and far, had made themselves present for the ball. The evening lasted much longer than expected and the musicians had to be asked to stay on for another hour or two to meet the pleasure of the crowd. The Viscount Mortel paid them well for the inconvenience and the players struck up their instruments once more with wide grins and heavy pockets.

The evening could not have been more of a success, the Baggingtons decided. The twins, who had spent the evening spinning about the floor with a near constant stream of partners, revealed that they even heard a remark that declared the family no longer worthy of the title "*the baggage*." Temperance could not care less what the masses called her, but she was pleased to know, for her brother's sake, that the reputation of the family was well on the way to redemption. In time, her brother would redeem the family seat and bring forth a new generation as the pride of the neighborhood. Of this she was sure.

She smiled thinking her little brother, Isaac had made this happen. It seemed strange to think of her little brother as a man, and stranger still that her new friend might hold a fondness for him. And what about herself? She was forced to consider. Did she hold a fondness for Teresa's brother? Certainly the moments in Mr. Crauford arms were like heaven to her. She felt none of the fear that a man's touch had so often generated.

She could not contain the smile that had taken over her features. Contrary to expectation, she had enjoyed herself the evening. Despite Lord Vardemere's best efforts, he had not been able to bring ruination upon her evening, or her life. Instead she felt exhilarated, and alive as she never had in the past. Mr. Crauford was the cause of her joy. Could he be her means to restoring her? And yet, could she subject him to damaged goods? For that was the crux of the matter. Here at home surrounded by her loving family Temperance's heart had begun to heal. Still, even if she found she could love a man after all she had seen, a gentleman as pure and good as Mr. Crauford deserved a bride who was the same. Not one such as herself. The thought pained her suddenly, but she had promised herself she would never marry.

When Temperance went to sleep that evening, she took off her shimmering blue gown and hung it where it could be seen from her bed. She remembered that her sister Prudence used to say that there were moments that she had wished that she could freeze in time for perfection. This was one such moment for Temperance. She closed her eyes and imagined the strong arms of Mr. Crauford surrounding her during their dance and for the moment she was content. She would not think of the future. She would only embrace now.

12

The following week was spent at the manor entertaining guests. The gentlemen explored the lands and rode horses across the newly manicured lanes while the ladies employed the pair of local female owners of the Nettlerush Tea Room to provide an elegant afternoon tea. Temperance did not recall the proprietors of the quaint shop and soon learned that they were new to the neighborhood, having established their business upon the widow's inheritance of her late husband's tea trade.

Temperance was pleased to taste the fresh leaves and sample the exotic scents that had once been so hard to come by in Upper Nettlefold. It did seem as if the neighborhood was expanding to become quite the stopping point for those of the gentry traveling between London and Bath.

The ladies made additional purchases from the offered selection, and even promised to visit the tea room before Miss Crauford, Mrs. George, and Lady Katherine made their departure.

Tea was hosted in the Mortel garden hall, a glassed room that was more menagerie than greenhouse as the Dowager Viscountess had long ago taken a liking to feathered pets. She once joked that she preferred birds to other animals solely because her husband had abhorred them. Temperance supposed that it was one way for her mother to establish a sanctuary in their tumultuous home. The Dowager Viscountess did not join them for tea as she had elected to remain abed for much of the afternoon. An evening of dancing had left her feet sore and swollen for she had stayed much longer than she had intended.

Amongst the faint chirping of birdlings and the scent of the last of the autumn blossoms in the air, the ladies spent hours recanting every detail of the previous evening.

"Robert said he should visit every year, now that your brother has opened the manor to leisure," Lady Katherine said of her brother. "It is a shame that such a fine house was kept closed off from the world for so many years."

"Yes, now the Lord Mortel shall need to secure himself a wife so that she might fill the halls to bursting with children and laughter," Mrs. Susan George added.

Lady Katherine offered a half smile and a nod of agreement. Temperance noticed the twin's shared look that confirmed her own thoughts, Lady Katherine had an inclination toward their brother Isaac.

"We should like nothing more than to become doting

aunts," Hope offered. "There will be no greater pleasure than watching our nieces and nephews grow into maturity."

Temperance pressed her lips together to avoid revealing the teasing nature of her siblings.

"Oh?" Lady Katherine seemed surprised and slightly off put by the prospect of the sisters remaining at the manor for years to come. "What of your own husbands and children?" she asked.

"We have no indications of marriage," Faith revealed. "Nor do we intend on searching them out."

"After all we have a pittance for a dowry," Hope added. "We shall be happy in our spinsterhood and keep entertained as we always have done." Hope took Faith's arm in her own.

"With each other," Faith added.

Lady Katherine's eyes grew wide at the thought that a lady might wish anything other than a swift and successful marriage. She kept her opinions to herself, though her resolution toward Isaac did seem diminished for the remainder of the meal. Temperance did not mind. Lady Katherine Dawson was entertaining enough and no offense had been had made for it was the twins that had set the prod. Still, she wondered if Isaac would have difficulty finding a match with so many unwed sisters to his care. Once again, Temperance wished to prevent becoming a burden on her family, though she agreed with the twins in their resolution not to wed. How would this affect Isaac's prospects? Few women would want so many sisters hanging on.

Temperance wondered if she too must find a way to

forge her own path, though she had no skill that would allow it except perhaps as a governess. She pursed her lips. Perhaps she should have remained at the Abbey.

"What is it?" Miss Crauford whispered with keen observation of her new friend's pensive look.

"It is nothing," Temperance replied. "It never occurred to me how a wife might look upon the many siblings, which fall under Isaac's care."

"Not to worry," Teresa replied with an unconcerned shake of her head. "Hope and Faith are far too appealing not to catch some fine gentleman's interest in time. Whether or not they might be convinced, is another thing. However, I can say, from the personal experience of a small family, that I would much rather have a dozen siblings to share my income than an empty house filled with nothing but coin and cold drafts. Lady Katherine was only surprised because she is the last of three daughters to wed and her mother has been about her for months to get on with it. It is more like that she is jealous of your freedom."

Temperance scoffed. "There is naught to be jealous of I assure you."

"What is it you two are whispering about?" Faith interjected with a pointed glare. "Do tell."

"We were only sharing secrets of our romantic encounters with dashing gentlemen this evening passed," Teresa said with a dramatic drawl. "I met a pirate in disguise and Temperance a sultan with fifteen wives who visited from afar. A shame that they had to leave England at first light else they might be found out by the Regent's guard and the manor would have been at siege."

The twins laughed and joined in on the fantastical tale. They imagined brooding captains who longed for a warm embrace and smart philanthropists who were in search of a partner for their good deeds. Soon, all of the ladies were laughing and the imaginary gentlemen became more and more ridiculous by the minute.

Never would such useless, albeit entertaining, conversation been permitted at the convent. Temperance allowed herself to give in to the pleasure, though her instinct was still to remain silent at meals. She had forgotten how one might be absurd with close companions and the simple joy that was elicited from the hearty laughter such imaginings induced.

"What is this?" A deep male voice said from the door that had been left open to the gardens. The gentlemen had returned and Mr. Edward George was staring down at the ladies as if they had lost their reason. The other gentlemen, smiled from behind his shoulder, all as amused as he at the silly game.

"We have all fallen prey to the pangs of love," his wife replied with a sly grin. "Engaged, the lot of us." Susan clapped her hands together as if the matter were settled.

"Engaged?" her husband laughed. "I am afraid that you shall have to decline your pirate love," the ladies erupted into laughter at his reference to their most recent creation, "and tell him that you have a husband and two small children to your name that require you home for supper."

"Fair enough," she heaved an overly dramatic sigh. "So long as the other ladies may keep their pleasure."

Isaac squinted at his sisters and shook his head. "Not

my sisters. A pirate shall never do." He feigned a resolute scowl. "The sultan has merit though. Perhaps he should take the lot. With fifteen wives already I doubt few more would be much trouble. However I had best receive at least one parcel each if I am to expand my fields before spring."

"To think," Hope turned to Faith with an expression of mock horror, "we are worth little more to our brother than graze land for a herd of cattle!"

So it was that the gentlemen pulled up their chairs and dispersed themselves among the ladies. More tea was brought and cucumber sandwiches passed around.

The remainder of the visit went on thus. Lighthearted banter passed among the collection of siblings and longtime friends. When it came time for the party to depart, Temperance was loathe to see them go. She had become especially taken with Miss Crauford, having grown to call Teresa her dearest friend and honorary sister. Temperance kissed her friend upon the cheek and promised to write. It had even been discussed that the Baggington siblings might spend the season with Teresa at her father's townhome in London. Temperance had always dreaded the London season but she felt all of a sudden that she might enjoy the celebration if spent among friends.

They said their tearful farewells. Lady Katherine offered one last lingering smile to the new Viscount Mortel before her own brothers lifted her into their carriage. Mr. and Mrs. George shared a carriage with Mr. Leeson and Mr. Fagean. Temperance realized she had not gotten to know Lawrence Fagean well during the visit, though he seemed friendly enough with the twins.

Lord Emery, was the last to leave as he was going in quite the opposite direction of the others. He sipped a glass of port before the ride. It might have been his third or his fifth. In any case, he declared that he should sleep the entire journey.

Temperance stood beside her siblings as they all waved farewell. All at once the manor seemed quiet and deflated. She missed the laughter and the lively music that had become the norm over the past days.

"Come now," Isaac threw his arm about Lucas's shoulders and mussed his hair. "No need for long faces. We shall fill the halls again before long."

"Do you mean it?" Hope asked with hopeful cheer.

"I promise you," he nodded. "I meant it when I said that there would be great changes moving forward."

This seemed to renew the spirits of his family, even the Dowager Viscountess seemed to want to press her son to set a formal date for the next event. He laughed and said that he would consider his schedule and that of the last of the reparations to the manor.

The others wandered inside, but Temperance remained to lean along the pristine marble rail that encased the steps.

When they were alone, her brother perched himself atop the banister as he had used to do when they were children and no one was watching.

"Did you enjoy yourself, sister?" he asked.

"I am surprised to say that I did," she admitted with a

smile. "Your friends are very kind. I enjoyed their visit very much."

"Excellent," he said with a nod. Isaac paused in such a way that Temperance could tell he wanted to say more but was hesitant.

"What is it?" she asked.

"It does me well to see my sisters enjoying themselves as they should have all these years." He shook his head with what she could only describe as disgust.

Temperance decided to tread lightly. As far as she had been made known, her brothers were unaware of the true plight of their sisters. That did not mean that Isaac had not observed that they had not been properly released into society, and had been kept much to themselves for many years. Perhaps he pitied them their isolation.

"We are most grateful for the... alterations that you have made to our home," she murmured in reply.

"I wish I would have..." he shook his head. "I wish things could have been different much sooner." He reached forward and grabbed her hands and held them in his own. "You know that you can always come to me, with anything you should require, as your brother and as your lord."

"I..." she hesitated. Was he asking her to reveal the truth? "I know, Isaac. I promise that, in the future, I shall always do so."

There, she thought. That was as safe of a gloss as she could manage in this difficult conversation.

"That is the most I can ask of you, I suppose," he said with a nod. "Just know that I would never... I would never let anyone harm my family." He paused, his face taking on a dour look that she never imagined on her younger brother's face. "Anyone," he repeated and his voice brought a tremor to Temperance's heart. Did Isaac know? How long had he been in possession of this knowledge?

Temperance swallowed deeply. She was reading into things in that were not there, she convinced herself. Of course this was the standard conversation that a new lord might have with a member of his doting family. It had, after all, now become his duty to provide and protect. Yet, Temperance felt as if there was a subtext that she was missing. She dared not ask more of Issac, lest he discover something of which he did not have previous knowledge. She thanked him again, avowed her confidence in his abilities as Viscount, and slipped back into the manor to ponder the strange conversation.

13

When Temperance could take wondering no more, she slipped her cloak about her shoulders and made for the road along the Nettlerush River. She could follow it to the village. Mrs. Cordelia Hardcastle had some explaining to do. She had no doubt that Mrs. Hardcastle was privy to all the secrets of the town, her own notwithstanding.

The Nettlerush River flowed with steady force from the recent rain, carrying fallen leaves and sticks along until they caught upon the edges of the banks and settled to their decomposition. Winter was nearly upon them. Temperance remembered winters of her youth at Mortel Manor. Depending upon the severity of the winter, the river might freeze and bold youths would race from one bank to the other upon their new skates, or couples might stroll hand in hand in the hope that a fall might allow for a brief embrace. The outdoor excursion with her younger siblings was a rare delight.

Temperance had used to love winter. The season in the Abbey had been hard to bear. Though the Masses were fine enough, and the sisters had done well to perform their acts of charity, there was little chance for excitement. The halls had been chilled and drafty, and the sisters soon grew irritated with the lack of changing scenery. Even nuns were human and prone to human frailty. Temperance found herself often praying for patience.

For that reason, she had come to love and value the last days of autumn. It had presented the opportunity for soaking up the final moments of pleasure as the weather turned. Even the air, as it did this day, had a crisp smell to it that could do nothing but bring joy to one's soul.

The walk to Nettlefold took less time than she expected, an hour at most. Her father had used to make it seem so very far, too far for the children to make the trip more than once a year. She shook her head. It was a fine, healthy walking distance: one that could be completed at regular intervals for the avid participant in exercise.

Temperance strolled down the street, not bothering to cover her face with her hood now that it was known that she had returned. Of course the gossip would have already circulated. It was a wonder how soon news might spread once the whispers had begun.

The gaping faces of the townsfolk stared after her. Gentlemen tipped their hats and ladies nodded their heads, but Temperance could only put a name to a handful of the passersby. She passed St. Cuthbert's Parish at the edge of the village just as the bells began to chime on the hour. It was almost as if they had struck to announce her arrival. Next, her path led her beyond the Bell and Whistle Inn and Nettlefold Arms. Neither establishment had ever been set foot upon by the Baggingtons for their father had often cursed the influx of travelers upon their town. He had been known to say that the filth had best pay their coin and leave for he wanted none of their interactions.

As she had grown in years, Temperance had begun to wonder if his real fear had been that his children would find friends and suitors and abandon him without hesitation. His sons had certainly done so at the first, and every, opportunity. His daughters would have followed suit if they had garnered enough acquaintances to make the leap for themselves, but he held them too close.

The door of Hardcastle House boasted a new wreath that had been trimmed with dried herb sprigs and evergreen fronds. Temperance smiled and gave the decoration a hearty sniff before she knocked upon the door. Simple luxuries were a particular joy to her now that she had gone without for so many years.

Mrs. Hardcastle seemed not surprised in the least to find Temperance waiting on her doorstep and ushered her into the parlor.

"Longer than expected," Mrs. Hardcastle mused, "though I suppose, with the ball, that you have been preoccupied."

"Then," Temperance furrowed her brow, "you know why I am here?"

"I have my suspicions..." Mrs. Hardcastle mused. "As, I am sure, do you."

Temperance's eyes grew wide. Would they jump right

into the meat of it? She had prepared herself for a quarter hour of formalities, at the least. Not, this direct address to the questions that were raging in her mind.

"My father's death," Temperance began. "Was it... natural?"

Mrs. Hardcastle took a deep breath and sank into her chaise. "What is it that makes you think otherwise?" the matron asked.

"Something that my brother said..." Temperance whispered. "That he would always... protect us. From... *anyone.*"

"A poignant statement," Mrs. Hardcastle nodded. "I have no doubt that he meant every word, but why should that concern you. It should give you peace of mind, should it not?"

"I believe," Temperance paused. This was not a matter to be taken lightly. Was she truly considering her own brother guilty of murder? A brother who had only been kind to her, when her father was so cruel. She supposed it was a consequence of her time at the convent. She felt compelled to ferret out the truth. "It was only, the way that he said it. Almost as if he were trying to tell me something," Temperance said weakly.

"Tell you what, dear?"

"Was my father's death natural?" Temperance repeated with resolve. She would not allow the question to go unanswered this time.

"Death from sudden illness is never the intended, natural, projection for one's life," Mrs. Hardcastle replied. "The only truly natural method of death is drifting away in the sleep of old age."

Temperance was impressed with Mrs. Hardcastle's verbal technique. The woman had neither answered, nor denied, any detail. Never for a moment would Temperance think that Mrs. Hardcastle had no knowledge of the situation. No. Temperance decided, she would have to be more exact in her questioning. If she wanted to know...Did she want to know? The words were out of her mouth unbidden.

"Was my father murdered, then?" Temperance rebutted.

"Goodness." Mrs. Hardcastle merely shrugged. "It is hard to say in such a case as this. Certainly there were many who wished death upon him." Mrs. Hardcastle wandered over to the mantle where her fingers trailed upon the wooden ledge in search of the offending dust that was like to be found. Her fingers remained clean. "I myself had many ill crossings with your father," she said with a far off look. "There are few in this town that have not. He was not well loved, as you know. In fact, he caused more offense in his foreshortened life than many might achieve in one of full length."

"Tell me true," Temperance crossed her hands and waited. "Did Isaac learn of his sins?"

"I shall say this but once..." Mrs. Hardcastle paused and gave Temperance a stern glare, "and then we shall speak no more of it... do you promise?"

Temperance nodded and leaned forward in anticipation.

"All that I shall say is that you were right in the assumption that your brothers were long unaware of the late Viscount's... fascination with his own daughters."

Temperance released the breath she had been holding. She had known it in the depth of her heart that her brothers would not have left their sisters to the monster all those years if they had known the truth. Yet what could they have done?

"They knew that you held no fondness for him, though neither did they, and so it was assumed that the Lord Mortel was not a favorite of any of his children. What with his temper, and all." Mrs. Hardcastle took a seat beside Temperance and enveloped the young woman's smooth hands in her own wrinkled ones. "I spent years attempting to convince your mother to tell the truth to your eldest brother, Isaac. It is only in light of the terrible events preceding your father's death that I believe she did so."

Temperance gasped. Her hand flew to her mouth to stifle the sound.

"I do not know what was said," Mrs. Hardcastle continued. "Nor am I certain whether or not he shared that truth with the others. Though such knowledge is certainly a terrible burden to bear."

Temperance wanted to ask more, but she got the impression that Mrs. Hardcastle would continue to be vague and evasive. She now had more questions than answers. Just what had happened while she had been away? Finally, after some time, Temperance spoke.

"If there has been foul play I understand that the less that I know of it, the better," Temperance said earnestly, fixing the elder woman with the full weight of her gaze, "but my desire for the truth is about much more than simple curiosity."

"You want to know if a mortal sin has been committed to forever damn another's immortal soul?" Cordelia Hardcastle asked. "Do you fear for your father's damnation?"

"Would you be surprised to hear me claim that I have no concern on that front?" Temperance offered with an abashed scowl.

"I would indeed," Mrs. Hardcastle seemed intrigued.

"I may have once thought I wished to be a nun, but there are several reasons that I was not suited to the vocation."

Mrs. Hardcastle remained silent as if awaiting Temperance's confession.

"If my father *was* murdered, I could not take the position of mourning for him," Temperance explained. "In fact, as you might assume, I find him worthy of the darkest pits of Hell. Mother Superior said that I should pray for the strength to forgive him, but I find cannot. That is at least part of the reason I never took my vows. I tried to pray for his immortal soul, but in my heart I am glad that he is gone."

Mrs. Hardcastle laughed outright. "Right you are." She pursed her lips and seemed impressed at Temperance admission.

"*If* something ill did befall him," Temperance continued, "I would also be loath to judge the one, or many, who might claim responsibility for such a deed. In fact, I might even be grateful to them, and that is not the outlook of a nun." Temperance bowed her head in shame and shook it as she wrung her hands at the admission of her own heart. "It is not a very holy viewpoint," she murmured. "I find that my greatest struggle was, and has always been, forgiveness." She looked up into Mrs. Hardcastle's eyes and saw her own confession reflected in the warm eyes of her companion. "I often wished for his death. For his damnation even. I prayed for it. I know that was wrong and sometimes I felt guilty for it, but I knew that if he would just disappear, then I might return home. I wished that his life would be cut short, but he was yet young in years and certainly set to live for many more with the robust history of our family's health. I never thought that it would truly come to pass. When I learned he had succumbed to some illness. It gave me hope and purpose. It renewed my strength and..." Temperance hesitated. "I cannot lie. It renewed my faith. It was an answer to my unspoken prayers and The Lord would not have allowed it if it were not His will, but murder cannot be the will of The Lord..."

"No, murder is not The Lord's will," Mrs. Hardcastle repeated in a dry tone. It was clear that she was merely parroting the Vicar's speech and Temperance suspected that, somewhere deep in the old woman's heart, she agreed with the inner sentiments of her guest. Men such as her father did not deserve forgiveness, and perhaps only The Lord was holy enough to grant it.

"Please, Mrs. Hardcastle," Temperance begged. "I must know the truth."

Mrs. Hardcastle groaned and pressed her face into her hands as if she must bolster herself for the reveal.

"Shortly after your father fell ill. Dr. Cedric Sharpton appeared here in a huff and asked me to join him for a tall drink." Mrs. Hardcastle began. "The

Doctor said he had his suspicions as to the nature of your father's death but had merely recorded it as the ague. Dr. Sharpton held no love for the Viscount and would shed no tear for his demise. Still, should he have performed a vivisection, he had wondered? I told him not to bother nor worry himself over it. If there was any evidence of foul play, you are right my dear, Isaac would be first to fall under suspicion and, true or not, that sort of rumor never leaves a gentleman's name. I merely persuaded Cedric to let it pass. Of course, he did not know that the truth of your father's *nature* and I was certainly not about to place that knowledge on the good Doctor's shoulders. I simply pointed out there was no cause to spend his time and effort on an investigation when there were none so terribly concerned about the matter."

Then Dr. Sharpton did think him tampered, Temperance wondered. How so? How might one make the appearance of an illness? Poison, Temperance thought. Though poison did not seem like her brother's method. No, he would have confronted their father direct.

Temperance tilted her head. "Why was Doctor Sharpton, excuse me for I do not know him, be so willing to overlook such a thing? Is he not an honest man?"

"Cedric is a cut above the rest," Mrs. Hardcastle assured Temperance. "He came to Nettlefold not too long ago now and has been a blessing upon our town ever since."

"But he hated my father... why?"

"Temperance... this isn't my tale to tell." Mrs.

Hardcastle argued, making one final protestation, but Temperance could tell she had nearly agreed.

"Please," Temperance begged. "I love my family and I am happy to be home, but so much has changed in my absence. Sometimes I still feel a near stranger here. If I am to move on with my life I need to know what has occurred."

Mrs. Hardcastle sighed deeply preparing herself to tell all. "Much has happened while you have been away," she began. "Much that, I am thankful to say, never made it to the gossip mills of the town."

Mrs. Hardcastle then broke into a harrowing tale that brought Temperance to her knees.

Mercy, always the quietest and most reserved of the Baggington daughters had been found with child this year past. The pregnancy had been easily covered because it had only lasted a few months. Doctor Sharpton had been called to save the girl when she had begun to hemorrhage without apparent cause. The child was lost and no word of the matter ever left the walls of the manor. The young gentlemen had been away at university at the time. Still Isaac had always been clever. He suspected the true cause of Mercy's condition, if not the source. He returned home demanding to know the name of the man who had dishonored his sister.

Dr. Sharpton had done his best to discover what gentleman was to blame for the lady's state as well, but Mercy refused to make the revelation. With her mother and father standing over her shoulder she remained resolute. Afterward, when the physician had arranged a moment alone, the best he could pry forth was that her aggington'scederic

father had given her a tea that he had claimed would soothe her. It was shortly afterward the bleeding had begun. Mrs. Hardcastle revealed that the Doctor had determined that the young Miss Baggington had been given an herbal remedy to end her pregnancy; her father's attempt to save his name and prevent any questions that might arise from the incident. Cedric had said that such potions were always a risky business and that two lives had very nearly been lost that day.

That, in itself, had raised the Doctor's suspicion as to the nature of the pregnancy. For Mercy's sake he had kept his own council, but from that moment onward he was resolute against the Viscount Mortel. Dr. Sharpton was a physician who was far ahead of his time and he had no tolerance for men of such ilk that called themselves *gentlemen*.

"Mercy has never spoken of any of this," Temperance said tearfully.

"I doubt she would. She would wish to put the experience behind her. I do think her troubles with her father diminished after the child. Put the fear of God in him it did."

Temperance doubted that her father feared anything, including God's punishment for his evil.

"Is their nothing left untainted by him?" Temperance wept for her sister's pain. "Must he ruin us all?"

"The twins I am fairly certain, have been left untouched." Mrs. Hardcastle said softly, in an attempt to calm Temperance's tears.

Temperance could not keep her mouth from falling

open. Could it be true? Had the twins retained their innocence? At least, in the physical sense

"Fearful, they may be." Mrs. Hardcastle continued. "Aware of what their sisters endured, I am certain. Without a doubt they anticipated his actions for years and that knowledge can cause its own sort of damage, but I do not think that he had yet worked up the boldness as to enter their joint room."

Temperance felt a small bubble of hope well up within her. The twins were spared. It did not take away all the terrible things that had occurred, but the black cloud cast by her father felt just a little brighter. Still, such tales did not quell her earlier suspicions.

"Did my...did my brother murder my father, then?" She said the last at a bare whisper.

Mrs. Hardcastle looked aghast. "Such thoughts from one who was almost accepted into a holy order," the elder replied with a wave of her hand. "Of course not."

Temperance felt her whole body relax. Surely it could not be true. Even if her brothers were pushed beyond endurance, they would not stoop to murder. Isaac would not. Not sweet Isaac. Temperance realized that Mrs. Hardcastle was still speaking. "It would be most ill-advised for the heir apparent to murder his predecessor. If it were allowed then some sons should off their fathers every day, I shouldn't wonder!"

Temperance was not consoled.

"But, if he died of natural causes," Temperance murmured. "Then I am to blame, my prayers, I..."

"No," Mrs. Hardcastle said firmly. "The Lord chooses

which prayers to answer. You must put any feeling of guilt to rest, now"

"I should have stayed." Temperance cried. "If had had never left then Mercy would not...It's my fault."

"No, child," Mrs. Hardcastle urged. "No, must not think that. We can never know what might have occurred but you cannot blame yourself." She raised Temperance tear streaked face to meet her kind gaze. "Neither you, nor any of your sisters, are to blame for your father's wickedness."

Temperance nodded mutely. The Mother Abbess had said much the same.

"How can you know all of this?" Temperance asked suddenly. Surely if the physician had been sworn to secrecy then Mrs. Hardcastle should not have known the sad tale.

"I am alone in my knowledge of the good doctor's concern," Cordelia continued. "But not from his mouth. Your sister, Mercy fell into melancholy and there was a fear that she might attempt to take her own life. The Doctor Sharpton convinced Lady Mortel to allow me to visit Mercy on a weekly basis, so that she might have someone to talk to...someone who understands such a loss."

Temperance sucked in her breath. She knew of what Mrs. Hardcastle alluded but she had never heard the woman make such a clear reference to the event. It had long been rumored that Cordelia Hardcastle had once lost a child of her own. Long ago, before she arrived in town and set herself up to become one of the most prominent women in Nettlefold. The details were unclear. She never spoke of it, but still the rumors persisted.

"Do you still visit Mercy?" Temperance asked softly gaining control of her emotions.

"I do," Mrs. Hardcastle said with a smile. "More often than not, she visits me now. We have moved on from the past and have become good friends. Someone to join for tea or a stroll is enough for her at the moment."

"It was very wise of Doctor Sharpton to make the connection," Temperance said with gratitude. "I am in your debt Mrs. Hardcastle. Your counsel most likely saved my sister's life, as it did mine."

Mrs. Hardcastle took the compliment with a sad smile. "I am glad to be of service to those in need," she said with a sigh. "I often wonder if I might have done things differently if I had had a strong shoulder upon which to lean in my own time of need."

"You've done wonderfully for yourself," Temperance protested. "How could you wish it different?"

"Oh, I have a great many successes," Mrs. Hardcastle replied, "but there are several things that I am lacking..."

Temperance had never heard the proprietress claim a want for a husband, or child, but she was fairly certain that that was what the matron was referencing.

"There is still time," Temperance assured her.

"Perhaps," Mrs. Hardcastle laughed. "If not for me, then certainly for you, Miss Baggington."

Temperance shook her head. "I have too much to think about with all I have learned this day to spare any thought for myself."

"Nonsense," Cordelia replied. "I would not have

shared the tale if I thought you would bottle yourself up and stow yourself away to collect dust. No," she said with firm resolve, "you must take the knowledge and make your peace with it. Permit that peace to be a balm to your soul. The harm is done. Your father is gone. Allow this chapter of your life to come to a close. There are blank pages ahead. Fill them with good."

Temperance gave a shaky laugh. She did not know how she might go about taking Mrs. Hardcastle's advice, but she promised the woman that she would give it her best. She thanked the woman again for all that she had done for their family. In secret, and without any recognition, Temperance had a feeling that Mrs. Cordelia Hardcastle had been the most powerful influence in all the changes that had come about for the benefit of the Baggington children. She did not know what would bring Mrs. Hardcastle to offer such friendship and devotion to apparent strangers, but she vowed that she would always be thankful for the woman. Temperance threw her arms around the matron's neck, an unusual gesture of affection that caught the woman off guard. After a moment, she accepted the embrace and gently laid her arms around Temperance.

A COLD RAIN HAD BEGUN TO FALL BY THE TIME TEMPERANCE returned to the manor. She and Mrs. Hardcastle had passed much time in conversation and Temperance had rushed back to the manor upon hasty feet to make her return before nightfall. Gibbons met her at the door, and this time, even in the pale dusk light he knew her face. She smiled and then realizing he probably could not see her expression, she put a hand on his arm and thanked him for his long service.

"'Tis no trouble, Miss," he said, but he sounded pleased with the compliment. Here was another man she could trust, she thought. Then she took a deep breath. She could not let her relationship with her Mercy remain broken, not after what she learned from Mrs. Hardcastle.

"Gibbons, do you know where Mercy may be?" she asked.

"I would imagine the library," he said, and Temperance shook her head. She knew that. Of course Mercy would be in the library.

Temperance paused at the entrance of the library. A candle flickered in the distance and a fire lit the closer books.

Seated in the corner with her nose a mere inch from the turning of pages was Mercy. The library had always been her sister's sanctuary. Without a word, Temperance padded over to where her sister sat upon the chaise lounge. Mercy did not look up.

"Mercy," Temperance said.

Her sister put the book aside and looked up at her but did not speak.

"Mercy, I want to help you," Temperance began.

"You cannot. What's done is done. At least he is dead now."

"He is gone, but your distress is not. You carry your pain like a shroud. You can barely look at me. Mercy please, I want to know my sister again." There was a long pause and Temperance spoke into the silence. "I spoke with Mrs. Hardcastle."

Mercy seemed to flinch. How could she ever forgive me? Temperance thought. Why would she? I deserted her to that monster, my own little sister. She wanted to gather Mercy into her arms. She wanted to make everything okay, but she could not.

Mercy just stared at her unmoved.

What she had endured...alone...it was unthinkable. Temperance sat looking into her sister's eyes. She could not speak. When she finally found her voice, she spoke through tears. "Mercy. I never knew, I mean I knew what could happen, but I had hoped..."

"For a miracle?" Mercy said.

A sob caught in Temperance's throat. She nodded. "I had hoped...for a miracle. I prayed for one."

"I received no miracle," Mercy said softly.

Temperance put her hand on her sister's. "I am so so sorry for what happened to you, Mercy. I know I should do penance for the rest of my days and it would still never be enough, only I beg you to forgive me."

Mercy looked shocked. "I don't blame you, Temperance." She said finally. "For a long time I did, but I understand now. You did all you could."

Now it was Temperance turn to look aghast. "But if I had stayed..."

"You would have been made the Lady Vardemere," Mercy interrupted. "You still would have been lost to me, just as Prudence was lost when she married Lord Fondleton."

Temperance shook her head in confusion "Then

why...?" She broke off leaving the question unspoken. Why had Mercy been so cold toward her since her return? If she did not blame Temperance why then was she avoiding her?

"Because I needed you, sister." Mercy whispered her own tears welling now. " I needed you and you were not here. Temperance I felt so alone."

Temperance held her sisters hand in her own and let her unburden herself

"When I found out, I went to Mother," Mercy said. "Before Mrs. Hardcastle." After a long breath she continued, with a quiver in her voice. "And then Father... figured it out."

Temperance closed her eyes. She squeezed Mercy's hand in sympathy.

"He wanted it gone," Mercy said at last, her voice a whisper. She paused and bit her lip. "I think I knew, when he gave me the brew...A part of me knew what it was. What it would do. I almost died. Sometimes I wish I had."

Temperance clutched Mercy's hand desperately, wishing she could help. "I'm glad you lived," Temperance whispered finally, tears streaming down her face. "I would have missed you terribly little sister."

Suddenly Mercy was in Temperance arms clinging to her like she had done as a small child. "Oh, Temperance I did miss you. Every night I missed you."

Temperance sank down on the chaise and pulled her sister's head against her breast as Mercy cried. Great wrenching sobs shook Mercy's body and Temperance wondered if her sister had ever let herself cry for all she had lost? Aimlessly Temperance pulled her fingers through Mercy's long hair, separating the tangles like she had done when Mercy young, before...before everything. Eventually Mercy's sobs died down. Still Temperance held her as if she would never let her go. Finally Mercy's breathing grew soft and regular. Still Temperance held her close and let her sister sleep safe in her arms.

Temperance filed all her knowledge away in the darkest recesses of her mind, knowing that it could never be spoken of. Still, it gave her a new appreciation for Mercy and for her family; for their struggles and victories. She thought about her brothers. She did not know for certain how her father had passed, but it did not matter. His fate was in the Lord's hands and for that she was grateful. She would never forget, but she was at last ready to let go of the past. She prayed Mercy would one day as well.

They were safe now. She knew her brothers were nothing like their father and she thanked God for that fact. She was able at last to pray in thanksgiving for her family. Never had she felt more loved than here with her sister tucked in her arms. She said another brief prayer for Mercy and for Mrs. Hardcastle who had changed both of their lives for the better. It was a wonder how much a single act of love and kindness could mean to a person.

14

---

*I*n the weeks that followed, Temperance felt a lightness begin to take hold in her heart. To learn that, like her friend Teresa, she had others that cared enough to look out for her wellbeing, was a revolutionary concept. So much of her life had been spent in fear, alone. She, like Mercy, was no longer alone.

The siblings began to take strolls about the village. The streets of Upper Nettlefold had never been graced with so many Baggingtons. They were greeted with smiles and queries as to the potential of another ball in the future. No longer were they shunned and snickered at from behind the coverage of cupped hands. Suddenly, residents of the neighborhood, even ones so prosperous as the Duke of Kilmerstan, the Earl of Rothlyn, and the great gossip the Baroness of Melfield, were making their greetings.

Eligible ladies came out in droves to look at the handsome, young Viscount Mortel and his handsome brother. Women whispered of the two younger Baggington brothers who were just as fine in feature.

Temperance found herself invited to a ride upon a phaeton, or a stroll about the park at Mortel Manor. She declined, of course, as she was not yet ready for such overt gestures of potential courtship. Still, the idea that she might be asked was a boon to her confidence. The compliment, well taken, brought a lightness to her step and a blush to her cheeks. It was so very different to have a gentleman approach with respect and offered interest, rather than being slathered upon or sold to the highest bidder.

A letter arrived at the end of the month from Phillip Crauford, the Viscount Pepperton, father to Evan and Teresa Crauford.

"A formal request for a visit," Isaac declared and he and Temperance walked along the lane behind the gardens. "They shall host a ball and have been so generous as to offer us invitation and lodging."

"Us?" Temperance asked in a breathy voice. She had never one gone for a visit to attend a ball. Isaac had, of course, many times over but for his elder sister it was a first.

"You and I," Isaac said with a nod. "It seems that Miss Crauford has taken quite a liking to you."

"Oh yes!" Temperance exclaimed that she was fond of Teresa as well. "It is only... Am I not a bit old to be making my first formal visit?"

Isaac shook his head. "Perhaps your experience is behind your years but you shall not be faulted for it. You did swimmingly at the last ball and I have confidence that you shall be caught up quick enough."

Temperance thanked her brother for his kind words and then begged that they might be off straight away.

"Of course," he laughed. "I have already sent our acceptance. I would not allow you to talk yourself out of it."

"You meddlesome fiend!" she giggled and made a playful slap at his arm. "Brother," she said with a sudden turn to a serious nature.

"Yes?" he asked with a cocked eyebrow.

Temperance raised herself to the tips of her toes and pressed a kiss upon his cheek. "Thank you for all you have done for our family. I am grateful to have you in my life," she said with a smile.

Isaac smiled in return and it occurred to Temperance that her brother still had a large burden to carry. Yet, he did so with a smile and his head held high. No further words were said, but it was clear that the siblings understood one another.

Then, with a peal of laughter, Temperance raced away to the manor to pack her trunk. They would not be leaving for several days but she must catalog her belongings and ensure that Miss Merton had time to fashion another of her masterful creations. Not a full gown, of course, but Dowager Viscountess Mortel had offered to have several of her own gowns, saved from the early years of her marriage, redone. Mary Merton had been adamant that she could bring them into the latest fashion. Though in such a rush, her skills would be tested to their limit.

THE CARRIAGE RIDE TO PEPPERTON HILL WAS A THREE DAY journey, a comparable distance to either London or Bath, though in quite the opposite direction of either. Isaac and Temperance traveled further into the country until the wood gave way to expansive fields and rolling hills. It was like something from a painting and Temperance wished that she could collect the image in her mind and savor it for all ages.

"The acreage at Pepperton is far greater than Mortel Manor," Isaac explained. With the lengthy history of the family seat, the generations of Viscounts had been wise enough in their investments to make continual advancements upon their holdings. "Evan has been a great source of knowledge as to how to restore Mortel Manor to its glory. The knowledge possessed between him and his father will save me years of guesswork and error."

"A fortunate friendship," Temperance mused.

"Evan is an old chum," Isaac laughed. "We got along from the off and he's a proper enough gent that I'd have liked him either way. Though, the connection is not one to scoff at. His father has resources that we could only dream of. Even the King's Counsel has written to request his knowledge on certain issues of note. They haven't met in person, of course, but the honor holds weight just the same."

"It certainly does," Temperance agreed. "I wonder that Teresa never mentioned it. I often find that such families have boastful tendencies."

"Not the Craufords," Isaac said with a scrunch of his nose. The gesture made him look young and Temperance was forced to repress a giggle lest she be forced to tell him that he looked like an adorable young boy in this moment. "You shall see, Tempe."

Having met two of the Craufords, Temperance was not sure what to make of her brother's statement. Teresa had said there were the only two children to their parents' names. Perhaps, he meant that the Lord and Lady Pepperton were a telling sort. All at once, Temperance felt both excited and nervous to meet them.

The Baggingtons were greeted at the door like honored guests by the entire Crauford family. Teresa rushed forward to greet her friend before Temperance's slippered feet even touched the cobbled drive.

"Mother, Father," Teresa turned with a proud smile. "This is Miss Temperance Baggington, and of course, you know her brother, the Viscount Mortel."

Her family laughed at her abrupt and disordered introduction, though no one cared enough to correct her. Introductions were made all around before they made their way to warm themselves by the parlor fire. A brisk chill had crept into the air and the threat of snow loomed ever nearer, but Temperance felt immediately flushed at the sight of Mr. Crauford.

"Come nearer the fire," he said, catching her hand. With his touch, she found herself in a cocoon of excitement. It was with effort she returned her attention to her friend, Teresa.

Temperance allowed Teresa to ramble on as they caught up on the news of the past week. Her mind, however, raced ahead with a series of thoughts all her own as Mr. Crauford regarded her with sparkling eyes.

His mother, the Viscountess Pepperton was nothing like Temperance had imagined. Though, what she had imagined she could not say. The assumption was that the lady of the house of such a prominent family would be larger than life. The Lady Pepperton was diminutive. Although, her dress was the latest fashion and showcased her slender figure with ease, the tip of her head only just broke the limit of Temperance's shoulder. In comparison to her towering husband she appeared a mere wisp of a thing. The lady's face was marred with a reddened blemish the color of port that covered one full cheek and a significant portion of her jawline and neck. Yet she was beautiful. Her features were warm and pleasant. Her bright green eyes had a soft, understanding tone to them that was endearing to all that fell within their scope. She had a soothing voice, like a tinkling chime upon the wind. Temperance liked her at once.

What was most notable about the lady had nothing to do with her person at all. It was her husband's treatment of his wife that caught Temperance's attention from the start. Lord Pepperton doted upon his wife. His affectionate gaze, always returned in kind, shone down upon his wife as bright as if they had only just discovered their love in that moment. His hand lingered upon her lower back whenever she stood at his side, and she often placed her own small hand upon his arm when she would look up to speak to him. Temperance had never been witness to such blatant signs of affection. Her own mother never touched her father unless she must and she did not ever remember her father touching her mother with affection.

"We are so happy to have you, Miss Baggington," Lady Pepperton said as she sat on the parlor sofa close beside her husband. "We have heard much about you these past weeks from both Teresa and Evan."

Temperance thanked the Lord and Lady Pepperton for the invitation into their home and declared her pleasure at having made their acquaintance. The quaint party sat and talked for several hours. Tea was served from the low table in the center of the room and Temperance decided that she far preferred this casual setting to a meal at the table.

She noticed Mr. Crauford was very attentive to both his mother and his sister as they spoke. Temperance found herself tongue tied, but Isaac conversed animatedly. At last Lady Pepperton turned to her.

"My son tells me you play the pianoforte," she said. "I would love to hear you play after supper," she said.

"I am afraid I am sorely out of practice," Temperance said. She did indeed love to play, but she was not ready for an audience. She felt her face flush with embarrassment.

"Mother, do not push. She has only just arrived." Mr. Crauford said saving her from further embarrassment, and Temperance threw him a grateful smile. "Both my mother and sister love Handel's music," he said.

The conversation revolved around music for the next moments, and Temperance relaxed.

"Well, we must be off," Lord Pepperton declared as he offered a hand to his wife. She took it and looked up into her husband's eyes with a loving smile. Together, they moved from the room and out into the hall with the promise of seeing their children and guests at supper that evening.

"I shall remain in your absence," Mr. Crauford said putting a hand on Teresa's shoulder.

The gesture clearly stating that he would keep a watchful eye on his sister while she was in the company of a young man not her kin. Temperance realized with a start that if Mr. Crauford was meant to be Teresa's chaperone, then Isaac was hers. Did she need a chaperone? She glanced up at Mr. Crauford a blush heating her face.

She wondered where the Lord and Lady Pepperton were off to. Her brow furrowed with confusion.

Mr. Crauford explained. "Mother and Father ride together most days, or as often as they can manage. In the warmer months, they ride horseback. In the winter, in an open sleigh."

"It's quite romantic," Teresa said with a sigh as she looked out the window to see the stable-master bringing a pair of horses up the drive. "They say the outings keep them young, but I think they just enjoy the time alone together."

"It is a remarkable tradition," Temperance said with surprise.

"You don't like it?" Teresa asked of her friend. She seemed shocked at Temperance's hesitant tone.

"Oh," Temperance shook her head. "I think it most interesting. It is only..." she looked to her brother with a small shrug, "I have never seen such a thing. Your parents appear still very much in love." She felt her face warm with a blush as she glanced at Mr. Crauford from under her lashes.

Now it was Teresa's turn to appear confused.

"Our mother and father were not what you would call, romantically inclined," Isaac explained with as much subtlety as he could manage. "In fact, they barely tolerated one another. Their marriage was not a happy one."

"Oh, what a shame," Teresa sighed. "You've never seen love expressed?" She asked.

"Only once," Temperance admitted shyly. "With my sister and her new intended... but those circumstances were... unique."

"Yes," Teresa nodded. "You said she had been widowed. What a shame that her first experience set such a bad record. I am glad she was able to find happiness in the end."

Temperance noticed that the gentlemen seemed uncomfortable with the conversation and so, with a laugh, she searched for something to change the topic. Besides, she thought, she had no interested in speaking of marriage.

"Tell me of your home," Temperance said, and Mr. Crauford took up the challenge describing all of the estate and the many tenants until the fire burned low. Not once did he say or do anything untoward, and Temperance found herself relaxing in his presence. Was it possible that a man could truly be a gentleman in manner as well as name?

"Perhaps we ought to go down to the edge of the lake

tomorrow," Teresa suggested with a turn toward Isaac. "You were fond of it, as I recall."

Isaac confirmed that he had enjoyed the scenery of the lake that fell in the center of the Pepperton properties. If it was warm enough on the morrow, Mr. Crauford suggested they could take a picnic.

"And if it is too cold, we can still ride around the water," Teresa suggested. Temperance hoped that the last of the warm weather held since she was not an accomplished horsewoman, by any stretch. She reminded herself she was among friends and there was no need for apprehension. Or perhaps Mr. Crauford more than a friend, she wondered as she lay in bed that night. She pulled the covers close and thought of his arms around her, sheltering her as they danced. She attempted to remember if there had ever before been a time when she had taken comfort in a man's arms. She did not believe so. Mr Crauford was the first.

15

The following morning the sun was shining. Although the air was cool enough for cloaks there did not appear to be a cloud in the sky. The gentlemen decided to take a pair of poles with which to fish while the ladies gathered blankets and pillows to make a comfortable seat. A small open chaise was loaded to carry them the short distance to the water and the party set off for their adventure. When they arrived, Mr. Crauford hobbled the horse beside the water and Isaac unloaded the blankets from the chaise. Temperance admired the lapping waves along the shore. Reeds and grass had lost their deep shade of green, but some of the trees still held their golden leaves. There was a beautiful and colorful bower along the water's edge. No wonder Isaac liked the spot. It was very picturesque. Temperance imagined falling asleep in the summer months to the sound of the rippling waters, stretched out upon bed of lush green grass, or reading a book beneath the ancient willow across the way.

Isaac cast his rod straight away, declaring that he would provide the evening meal from the depths of the water. Teresa giggled and threw out her brother's line in the opposite direction with a declaration that she would best the avid fisherman.

"It's always a competition," Evan Crauford laughed as he watched the pair at their banter. "Teresa takes great pleasure in fishing and is often in need of a gentleman or two as an excuse to enjoy the sport."

"Who usually wins?" Temperance asked. She flung out one of the blankets. Mr. Crauford grabbed the opposite corners and helped her to lay it flat.

"It is a toss-up," he laughed, "but gentlemen seem to be flummoxed when they are out-fished by a slip of a girl."

"Then you should try!" Temperance pressed.

Mr. Crauford shook his head and continued to help her settle the lounging area. "Oh I know Teresa can best me," he said. "Anyway, we only brought the two poles. One must have gotten broken when the stable boys borrowed them the other day."

"It's a shame that you have to miss out."

Evan shrugged. "I've no complaint against watching," he said, taking her hand and Temperance flushed. She was once again cognizant of the fact that Mr. Crauford was not an adequate chaperone, and certainly her own brother was more interested in Teresa than in chaperoning his sister.

"Besides," Mr. Crauford said. "That pair has enough fun for all of us."

It was true, Temperance realized. Isaac and Teresa were laughing and had barely taken note of their siblings' presence. Teresa's face would turn up to the young Viscount and then she would look away before he might catch the glance.

Temperance smiled. Teresa's crush was, without a doubt, her brother Isaac.

"What is it?" Mr. Crauford asked upon noting her expression.

"Nothing," Temperance shrugged. She did not know if the gentleman was aware of the flirtations going on before them, but she dared not point it out.

"They don't flirt in public," he whispered after a short while noticing her gaze. "Only when they know nobody is watching."

"We're watching!" Temperance exclaimed with a squeak, surprising herself.

"We don't count," he replied. "I've grown used to it over the years, though it is only in recent months that they've come to ignore me as well." He laughed with good nature. Temperance was glad to see that he was not offended.

A chill breeze whipped through the air and Temperance shivered. Mr. Crauford grabbed the last of the blankets from the carriage and held it open so that she might wrap it around her shoulders. She turned and offered her back and the fabric was draped with so gentle a touch that she should have hardly felt a thing, but she was aware of his every movement, his every touch. The thought brought butterflies to her stomach but no fear.

She settled herself amongst the pillows and tucked her feet beneath her. With the blanket draped so, her entire body was protected from the wind, save her head. She could feel her cheeks growing rosy but did not mind. It was more a result of the fresh air than the chill or perhaps her flush was due to the proximity of the gentleman beside her. She was not sure. She had never felt so about a gentleman.

Evan settled down on the far side of the blanket and leaned on one elbow to prop himself against the pillows. His jacket pulled across his chest as he settled himself. She could feel the heat of him beside in the cool afternoon and wondered what it would be like to be held close her head pillowed on his broad chest. She looked away, her face filling with heat.

She kept her face turned toward the pair of lovers by the lake though she could sense that Mr. Crauford was watching her expression. How had she overlooked Isaac and Teresa? Mr. Crauford had said that they were muted in public, but still, Isaac was not one to bestow his affections wildly. There must have been signs that he had a preference. Still, she could recall none. She turned back to Mr. Crauford as her face cooled. He was smiling at her.

"You appear quite at your leisure," Temperance observed.

Again he shrugged; completely at ease with his surroundings. "I like it here," he said in reply, "with you." He laid his hand over hers like a question and

Temperance allowed him to close his fingers around her own gloved digits.

"It is very peaceful," she replied. She looked up into his dark eyes. "I like it too," she said, and the moment held between them, her brother and Teresa forgotten as he tightened his hand on hers.

The moment was broken abruptly as Teresa let out a victorious shout, the tip of her pole bent near to the water. She cried out in excitement as she skillfully brought the sliver creature to shore and pranced with excitement as Isaac removed the fish from the hook and tossed it into the empty basket.

"Did you see that?" Teresa turned with a beaming grin to Temperance. Temperance clapped and cheered for her friend, reluctantly reclaiming her hand.

"Hey!" Isaac feigned an angry tone but could not contain the look of pride in the lady that bounced with happiness at his side. "You are supposed to be on my side, Tempe."

"My apologies," Temperance giggled then offered a pained expression. "I suppose you shall have to partner Mr. Crauford. Gentleman against the ladies."

Mr. Crauford gaped at her and Isaac near bent over with laughter. Temperance was overcome with laugher and buried her face in her knees to stifle the sound.

"Not a fair trade," she could hear Isaac wheeze. "Come on, Ev, it is not fair that a lady is so skilled at fishing. Tell your sister to allow me a gentleman's pride."

"I can no more control her than I can control the weather," Mr. Crauford replied smoothly. "Your disappointment at the loss shows bad sportsmanship. A true gentleman would concede defeat to his betters."

Isaac pretended to be offended for all of two minutes before he fell back into conversation with his female companion. The fisherman and lady returned to their task with renewed focus. The game was afoot.

Temperance was surprised at how easy it was to converse with Mr. Crauford. There was no flattery or overbearing compliments. In fact, they merely stated the facts of their interest until they discovered that they held one very substantial thing in common. A love for music.

"I never heard you play when we stayed at the manor," he said with an unhappy expression.

"I could not have done so," she replied with her best attempt to pretend it was no matter. "The music hall was emptied sometime whilst I was away as you well know. There are no longer any instruments to play."

"The loss of your instruments was criminal." Mr. Crauford stated with a look of abject horror. "Music halls were often the collection of generations and the pride of a family."

Temperance nodded. "My father was... angry at me, I think," she whispered. "I am sure it was meant to be a punishment."

"For not marrying that rat, Lord Vardemere?" he spat with anger in her defense.

"Mostly," she said with a nod. "As well as for running away. I suppose I deserved it."

"Do not say such things," Mr. Crauford catching her hands in his. "No one deserves punishment for refusing a marriage. Besides, he didn't just hurt you; he destroyed the pleasure for any others that might follow. 'Tis a shame, surely, but you must not blame yourself. Dramatic behavior meant to hurt someone only succeeds if they permit themselves to feel hurt." He brought both of her hands to his lips and kissed one and then the other. She could not breathe at his gentle touch. She completely lost the thread of the conversation and simply watched his lips as he spoke. "You must not let your father's petty actions bring you sadness. You must rise above and refuse to allow it to upset you. Only then will you defeat him."

"I never thought of it that way," she mused.

"Therefore, you must play again."

She nodded. "Still, I have forgotten more than I have remembered. I shall have to start from the beginning."

"It can be done," he said. "A new beginning with a new purpose."

"Yes," she said realizing that he had given her that new purpose, and she was not only thinking of music. Prior to meeting him she has been but drifting through life, unsure of herself, but he had such verve and vitality that she could not help but be swept along. Now she wanted to find new beginning, with Mr. Crauford.

"I do believe that it can be done." She thanked him for his thoughts on the matter.

Temperance realized Mr. Crauford had, in a remarkable short span, reminded her that she had promised Mrs. Hardcastle to find pleasure in life and devote herself to it. She had once loved music. She still did. She would no longer allow her resentment of her father, and his attempt to destroy her pleasure, to keep her from it. Perhaps, in time, she might convince Isaac to purchase a small harpsichord. She would not be so presumptuous as to ask for an item as expensive as a pianoforte or a harp, but it would give her great pleasure to play again. Her father was gone. She would no longer allow him to cloud her happiness.

"It's settled then. You shall begin tomorrow," Mr. Crauford said with a wink.

"Tomorrow?" Temperance murmured. It was only then that she realized he still held her hands in his, and the heat of his hands seemed to sear through her gloves straight to her heart.

She was confused by his pronouncement but he would reveal no more. The anticipation of the morrow thrilled her for the rest of the evening. What could he mean by it? Better yet, the longing to make music brought a joy to her heart that she had long forgotten. Was it only longing for music that filled her, she wondered. Or was the longing in her heart for Mr. Crauford himself?

She watched him, his eyes bright with laughter as he stared into hers. He released one of her hands and brought his fingers up to cup her chin. In a moment, her eyes fluttered closed and his lips brushed hers, so lightly, so gently, but there was a heat there that bubbled through Temperance's entire being with only the softest touch

"Ho Ho! None of that," called Isaac.

And Temperance looked up suddenly, her face filled with the fire of embarrassment. Apparently Isaac was a better chaperone than she had first thought.

Isaac chuckled. "That's my sister, Evan," he said. "I shouldn't want to call you out."

Isaac's tone was jovial but his eyes were serious as he looked questioningly at Temperance. She smiled at her brother and at Mr. Crauford projecting a feeling of ease and Isaac relaxed. She was safe among friends but it warmed her to know her brother would defend her should she ever require his aid.

Mr. Crauford stood and Temperance offered her hand allowing him to guide her to her feet. "And what of my sister," Mr. Crauford said. He gestured lightheartedly toward Teresa who looked a bit disheveled herself, holding the basket of fish.

"Isaac did not catch a single thing," she exclaimed, her eyes shining brightly.

"Oh I think he did, sister." Mr. Crauford said, and the group burst into laughter.

"As long as the lady has no complaint," Isaac said, "I suppose I needn't call you out, Evan, but you must remember my Tempe is a delicate flower. She was after all very nearly a nun."

The group laughed again as they gathered the blankets and hitched the horse again to the chaise and returned home. Temperance's lips burned with the memory of Mr. Crauford's kiss. She had never thought the touch of a man would bring her joy, and now, she did not know what to think at all.

16

*A*fter the morning meal, the house was abuzz with preparations for the ball. Issac and Temperance had arrived the day before, as requested, but were told that they were not allowed to lift a finger to the aide of the hostess for Lady Pepperton had all the preparations well in hand.

"Come," Mr. Crauford gestured down the hallway so that his companions might lead the way. "Your surprise awaits." Teresa bounced along with an excited giggle.

"I simply cannot wait!" She exclaimed. The young Miss Crauford shared a knowing glance with Temperance's brother. Their smiles revealed that they had been informed of Evan's surprise. Temperance had not. When had Mr. Crauford had the opportunity to share the secret?

"Why is it that everyone else might know, save me?" Temperance complained.

"Because you shall take the most pleasure in the

surprise," Isaac replied with a gentle pat to his sister's head.

Temperance gave a huff and crossed her arms below her breast, refusing to walk any further until she had been told what sort of plot was afoot.

"Come now," Evan repeated. "I promise that it shall be worth your discomfort." He looked down upon Temperance's nervous form with a comforting glance that gave her confidence. It was not that she meant to be difficult. It was only that, in her experience, surprises did not bode well for the recipient.

"Will you not trust me?" he asked and she looked up at him. His eyes were shining with pleasure, and she thought, she did trust him, more than she had ever trusted a man. He caught her hand and squeezed it gently. "Come," he said, and she clamped her lower lip between her teeth and followed in the gentleman's footsteps.

When he stopped to stand before an elegant, stained glass door, she could not explain why but she trembled in anticipation. She was both excited, and fearful. The best that Temperance could come to describing her feeling was to say that somewhere in the pit of her stomach she felt a nervous anticipation. It was good sort of anticipation, yet it was an unfamiliar feeling Temperance. She had become accustomed to anticipating hardship not pleasure, and yet the fire in Mr. Crauford's eyes certainly suggested pleasure. She shivered with excitement and he smiled at her as he put his hand on the opaque doors and opened it to the room beyond.

What she beheld left her standing frozen, as if in a dream, just inside the threshold. The room was far longer that it was wide and seemed to go on ahead of her a great distance so that the door at the far end seemed nothing more than a door which might be used for child's play. Her breath caught in her throat and she could not speak. Her heart palpitated something terrible, almost painful in its beating as she looked upon the beauty within.

She turned to stare with wide eyes at Mr. Crauford. She could see that he was awaiting her response, but she could hardly move save for the turning of her head and the repeated opening and closing of her mouth.

"What is this place?" she said upon the only breath she could muster.

Evan laughed. "You know exactly what it is," he replied.

It was by far the most elegant music hall that she had ever laid eyes upon. The room was set out from the rest of the building so that two walls were made of windows that let in the light of the sun or the moon depending on the time of day. She assumed now that the double door at the far end of the room would open to the out to the garden and imagined them being flung wide to allow a sweet summer breeze to trickle in. Presently a cheery fire roared to her left filling the room with warmth.

Temperance had never seen so many instruments in one place. She noticed two pianofortes. Stands filled with hanging chimes of varying sizes were strewn about the room accompanied by a range of harpsichords. Small tables were covered with a variety of smaller instruments, from lutes and harp-lutes, to violins and overlarge viola, even a clavichord. There were a number of instruments that she did not recognize. Spread about on various tables was sheet music of all sorts.

"Go on then, enjoy," Mr. Crauford said and Temperance looked up at him as her brother and Teresa came up behind them both.

Her brother laughed. "Have at it, Tempe."

"Oh, Isaac," Temperance wrung her hands together to keep them from flying to their loves, "I have not played in an age. I am sure that I have forgotten how."

"Impossible," Teresa declared. "Isaac tells me you were better than any concert pianist he ever heard."

Temperance felt a blush rise to her cheeks. "That was a very long time ago."

"I hardly believe that you never played at the Abbey," Mr. Crauford pressed. "I know they have an organ for services. Surely you played."

"Yes. The good sisters oft allowed my fingers to pluck the keys at a service," Temperance acknowledged with a telling shake of her head, "but those hymnals had nothing of a concerto to them. It was more simple notes to accompany the cantor at Mass."

"We shall not think harsh thoughts if you plunk about a bit of tune at first," Mr. Crauford led her into the room. "The memory shall not return until you begin."

Temperance's hands wished for nothing more than to fly across the ivory keys of the grand that had caught her eye at once. With tentative steps she approached the instrument and brushed her fingers along the hand carved panels that had been inlaid along its length. Imaginative scenes of fantastical beasts, celestial beings, and even the excitement of a stag hunt were crafted with intricate care so that they stood out from the wood as if in an attempt to come to life. The finest of brushes had painted their likeness so that the piano was a work of art before a single note was played. It seemed a shame to even open the cover and seat herself beside such a beautiful instrument.

Teresa leaned forward and laid her head upon the lid so that she might both hear and feel the vibration of the notes as Temperance began a simple melody that was first taught to children.

"Evan and I used to lie upon the lid for hours while mother played," she crooned.

"You did not!" Temperance gasped and her fingers screeched to an abrupt halt. To think that a pair of children might have climbed upon the magnificent instrument and risked its damage was beyond her comprehension.

"Mother is very fond of music," Teresa explained. "As are we. It made for pleasant memories." When she saw Temperance's mortified look she laughed. "We stopped when we grew too large for the practice."

The music hall at Mortel Manor, when it had existed, had been nice enough but certainly not a place where childish antics would have been permitted. Temperance had been allowed to play for one hour each morning and evening. Serious study and practice were all that had been allowed. Though she had found her own pleasure in it, music had never had a place in family gathering or fond memories, and she said so.

"I remember your playing with fondness," Isaac said,

and Temperance looked at him. "As a child I often awoke to it in the morning. I would lie abed and listen."

"You never said so," she murmured.

"I know it is difficult to imagine," Isaac said. "One thing that took me a very long time to make sense of, Tempe, is that our friends have had a *very* different upbringing than ourselves. Their house was filled with light and happiness. Music and... and fun! That is part of the reason that I thought you must come to see for yourself. The world is not at all as we have known...as you have known. There is light and happiness here."

Temperance shook her head with wonder. To hear her brother say so made the idea more believable. She could not imagine a childhood such as the Craufords had described. Yet, for some it must have been real.

Again she feathered her fingers over the keys and a tune surfaced in the back of her mind, one that she had forgotten but only just remembered as her fingers moved over the keys.

Slowly, she began to pick the tune from her mind and test the keys to match. Here and there her fingers or her memory would stumble and she would have to start again, but she kept at it with singular focus.

Evan offered a hand to his sister and twirled her toward the center of the hall. Teresa giggled and again Temperance was amazed at the bond that the small family shared. There was no artifice or effort to it, just a natural connection and appreciation. Isaac sat upon the edge of the bench beside Temperance and watched the dancers while he listened to his sister play.

"You like her, don't you?" Temperance asked. She

dared not look up from the keys yet. The movement and spacing was still unnatural to her ill-used hands. Still, she could not halt the slow spread of a smile from crossing her face as her fingers stroked the ivory keys.

"What?" Isaac turned with an expression of surprise. "We are good friends."

Temperance pursed her lips and set back to her music. She did not believe her brother's evasion, but if he was yet unwilling to admit the truth of his heart she would not push him. Perhaps friendship was the first step towards love. She knew better than most that the mountains that must be scaled and the fears overcome before such an issue might be addressed.

"Just friends?" Temperance asked softly.

He sighed. "I have been friends with her brother for so long I am sure she thinks of me as another brother."

"I do not it think so," Temperance whispered, and she glanced at her brother to see a light in his eyes.

Mr. and Miss Crauford moved further away and though their laughter carried throughout the music hall, until their conversation was out of reach at the far side of the room. Temperance fell at once in love with the format of the room. Its long, thin style meant that the music could be heard throughout without the musician feeling under the eye of her audience. At home, the room was elegant but small enough that she had always felt a bit nervous and crowded if the others were within. This room had been built for music, and for the love of it. She closed her eyes and imagined how the change of weather outside the many windows might even affect the mood of the place. The surroundings were such a feature that she could only dream of the type of music that her heart might bring forth during a dense snowfall, or better yet, during a light summer rain, or the current stark conditions outside. Nothing else was necessary. A heart could be content with nothing more than this room, she thought.

Mr. Crauford had bestowed upon her the greatest gift. To allow her even a moment to savor his mother's music hall was more than she could have ever wished. Nothing would ever compare.

After a time, Isaac stood from the bench. Its low groan warned her of his absence so that she might chance a look up to see him making his way toward the dancers. With a low bow and a sweeping hand he took possession of Miss Crauford and settled her within the frame of his arms so that she might now dance with him.

Temperance bit back another smile and focused her attention back to her notes, with a twinkle in her eye. After a moment's thought she blended one tune into another until, rather than a lively march, she transitioned into a slow and romantic waltz. Her brother might curse her for it later, she thought, but for now he appeared happy with her choice. He drew Teresa into his arms and whirled her around the room. Teresa looked ecstatic. Temperance turned from watching the dancers to realize that Mr. Crauford was watching her. She blushed and looked down, but the man was not to be disavowed.

Mr. Crauford made his way back toward the ornate pianoforte and pulled up a chair beside Temperance's bench. He was not so bold as her brother who had sat alongside her as she played. Of course, she thought, she was only just beginning to know Evan Crauford. A gentleman such as he would not be so forward after such a short time, and yet, he had kissed her; what could be more forward than that? A shiver ran through her at the thought.

"I do not know how I can ever thank you for this gift," she offered after she began to grow a bit more confident in her play. Isaac had been right; it was coming back to her. Slowly, but soon enough and with practice she would regain her talent.

"There is no need for thanks," Mr. Crauford replied. "These instruments are meant to be played. You do us well to allow us the pleasure of enjoying your music."

"I would not go so far as to claim that much," she laughed. "I am still fumbling my way about. In time, however, I should like to try again." She looked up with a hesitant glance. Would he invite her to visit again? Would she be allowed to play in this wonderful hall once she had practiced a bit?

"As often as you wish," Mr. Crauford promised. "I shall ensure the doors are left open every day during your stay. You may play as often as you wish. I only ask that I may be present on occasion to enjoy your music."

"Thank you," Temperance replied. She could not help but feel sad that this visit may be her only. Something about this place and this family felt like a balm on her soul.

"And of course you shall have to visit us again before long. My sister has blossomed in your friendship. She is usually quite shy. She would stick to my side, but no more. Now, she is off wherever you might be." He sounded cross but when Temperance looked up to see his expression she saw that he was teasing her. "I am glad that she has found a friend. A woman without sisters needs such companionship, and I cannot offer it to her."

"I do not think it is my presence Teresa enjoys most," Temperance whispered with a coy smile.

"Of that there can be no doubt," Mr. Crauford laughed as he glanced at Isaac and Teresa with their heads together, "but there can be no mistaking that she values your friendship as well. There is no falsehood there."

Temperance nodded and agreed. She knew from the first that their friendship was to be real and lasting. Still it was fun to tease the pair about their unacknowledged romance.

"You seem different when you play," Mr. Crauford observed after a time. "It is as if whatever weight lives upon your shoulders might float away on the sound of the notes."

"Sometimes it feels that way," she agreed. "Or at least I wish it would."

Mr. Crauford grew serious at once. "Tell me what troubles you Miss Baggington, If I may make it right I shall at once."

She shook her head, shocked that he would care for her troubles. Still, she could not speak of such things. She may never speak of them. Instead of revealing her melancholy, she chose to speak of music instead.

"There is something soothing to the art. I never could get it out of my mind. Sometimes it feels like I could express myself through the notes better than I might ever with words."

"Try now," he said with an encouraging lean forward.

"Oh, I couldn't," she laughed. "I am far too out of practice to play on a whim." She had used to simply sit down and play whatever her heart felt. Now, she did not feel so familiar as to be able to create anything other than what had been memorized or copied from a page.

"Close your eyes," he instructed. "Play what you feel."

Temperance cast him a hesitant look and then, with a deep breath, she closed her eyes and continued to play along the piece of her memory. She did not want to give the dancers a reason to stop their stroll. Slowly, she thought about how she felt. She thought about all of the feelings that she had felt in the course of her lifetime and tried to isolate what it was that she was feeling in this moment.

A soothing melody sprung forth. Gentle ebbs and flows reminded her of the elegant beauty of the dancers, the room and the surrounding countryside. It was a happy tune, but with a hint of sadness as well. Not, because she was sad, she determined, but because there was an undercurrent of longing that she could not fully understand. She did not want to think about it further, and so she turned her thoughts to a lively romp across a field and let the music follow. With her eyes closed she could imagine the bounce of a horse beneath her as it leapt a small stream and began to race at a breakneck speed across the meadow.

"What are you thinking of?" Evan asked with amusement.

"A horse chase," she peered at him through the slit of one eye. He nodded and she continued on.

"Another," he pressed.

Her fingers drifted into the pitter patter of a spring rain. The fine dripping of morning dew as a fog rolled across the field. Here, she imagined herself looking out of a window with a roaring fire to her back. It was both serene and ominous. One never knew when a storm might turn and yet, they were beautiful to watch as they gathered in the sky and tumbled across the English hills.

"A tempest!" he cried.

"Not quite," she laughed. "A simple rainfall seen through the windowpane."

"I thought I heard thunder," he argued. She thought it funny that he would argue with her own musical images but, he was right.

"There was thunder," she said with a nod, "but far off in the distance and no danger to me, with only a flash of light here and there to illuminate the sky."

Evan scooted his chair closer and Temperance could feel the heat of him at her back. She cleared her throat and squeezed her eyes shut. She had no doubt that he was watching her with his piercing gaze.

"...and now?" he murmured, his breath in her hair.

Her heart leapt in her chest and Temperance felt all at once covered with a fever. She did her best to turn her mind away from the gentleman. She did not know why it was that she was flustered, and she refused to analyze the sensation. Her traitorous mind turned to the near-lovers that floated across the hall a short way away. Her tune slipped into a romantic amble. A slow and tenuous ache of the heart was prevalent in the keystrokes. Temperance threw herself into the music, determined that it was written for Isaac and Teresa alone, but she could not think of her brother and play. Her mind kept drifting to the man at her side, to the touch of his hand and his lips upon hers, his breath in her hair.

"I like this one," Mr. Crauford murmured after having sat silent for so long that Temperance leapt a bit at his voice but continued to play on, her fingers fumbling before her mind renewed its focus. "What are you thinking of?" He asked softly.

She pulled her hands away from the instrument as if she had touched a hot coal. She could not speak of it.

"That was beautiful," Teresa called and continued to hum along as she made her way back toward the seated pair with Isaac in tow. "I wish it had not ended."

"I share the sentiment." Evan agreed, his deep tenure rolling over Temperance skin. "Miss Baggington, you are a delight."

Temperance thanked Mr. Crauford for his compliment while looking at his shoes, unable to make sense of what she was feeling. She was grateful for Teresa's chatter because it gave her reason to ignore the lady's brother and avoid an answer to his earlier question. What was she thinking of? She could not answer truthfully. She could not say she had been thinking of him. It would be too forward, and yet she thought that somehow he knew, just as he known there was lightning in the previous sequence.

Renewed from her dance, the young Miss Crauford was ready to show their guests about the estate. She pulled Temperance from the bench and began the tour with animated gestures and lighthearted jokes about her family's history. Isaac and Mr. Crauford followed smiling.

"One of the benefits of having one of the oldest seats in the country was that there was always ample knowledge of generations past," Mr. Crauford commented. The Craufords had been collecting tales and relics to pass down for years. It soon became apparent from Teresa's commentary that the entire family was good natured, except for one great-uncle Roderick who was run through for his cantankerous ways by a gent at a tavern one night. Humor abounded and Temperance wished to know more about every painting and statue that adorned the expansive halls. She realized she wished to know more about Mr. Crauford.

17

The remaining days leading up to the ball were much the same. The two ladies and two gentlemen were inseparable from dawn until dusk learning about one another. Even if they resolved themselves to quiet reading by the firelight, they were never far apart. Temperance began to grow more and more used to the comfort of her companions, but she could not deny that she had made a concerted effort to keep her distance from Mr. Crauford, lest she form an attachment. She began to suspect that Evan had even caught on to her avoidance.

The ball arrived in collaboration with an icy rain. The skies had not yet committed themselves to a blustery snowfall, but the near attempt was enough to foretell the promise of winter.

"Will all still come in such weather?" Temperance wondered aloud as she fixed the neat curls of Teresa's hair.

"Without a doubt," Miss Crauford replied. "There is nothing this neighborhood loves more than a party, except perhaps a ball! Not a soul should dare to stay at home when there is fun to be had." Teresa went on to explain that her parents threw legendary balls and picnics. Guests would travel from miles around just to enjoy a few hours of their entertainment. Some, would even post up nearby for the night at an inn or some such posh establishment. The extra cost would be worth the addition of a few hours at Pepperton Hill. "But only the most favored were invited to stay at the hall," Teresa said with a smile at Isaac.

Temperance heard a foot on the stair and turned.

"Darling, you look more beautiful with every passing day," a deep voice spoke from the upper floor and Temperance smiled to see it was The Lord Pepperton who had spoken. The Viscount was making his way down the staircase, his lady on his arm. He stared lovingly down into her eyes and continued to offer sincere compliments. Temperance could hardly believe it, but the lady blushed a color nearly matching the port wine stain on her cheek. After years of marriage, she still blushed at the flattery of her husband.

Temperance had been taught to believe that beauty was fleeting. That a husband might take a fancy but grow weary as age diminished a woman's charm. One might think that the Lord and Lady Pepperton had only just begun their romancing. Though, from the age of their children, she knew that they had married nearly three decades. Still, their sentiment remained.

Teresa noticed that Temperance was staring and leaned close to whisper into her friend's ear.

"Neither Evan nor I will settle for anything less than the love of our parents share," she murmured. "Is that not how marriage should be?"

Temperance nodded but could not seem to form words as the pair made it to the landing and continued to dote upon one another. Their affection was not for show. Lord Pepperton did not offer a well-timed compliment for the benefit of the room and then turn his back upon his wife. He kept her tucked neatly under his arm as if he could not bear the thought that she might leave his side. Lady Pepperton leaned into her husband, soaking in his protection and strength.

"Dozens of ladies have vied for Evan's hand and, though he has tried, he cannot seem to fall in love with any of them." Teresa whispered.

"What a shame," Temperance replied. "Perhaps his expectations ought to be readjusted."

"Not at all," Teresa murmured. "There could have been no affection with any of them when it was painfully clear that they were only after his position and income. A woman like that could never trick Evan's heart. He is too steadfast and logical." Teresa stared off in the distance with an idyllic grin. "We will know when it is true. That is what mother always says. When it happens... there can be no doubt."

"Is that the way you feel about Isaac?" Temperance asked with a sudden bold leap.

Teresa's face turned bright red and she shot a sidelong look at the young Viscount Mortel.

"Sometimes I think it could be," she admitted shyly. "Though, I cannot yet say for certain. You cannot ever *really* know love until you give in to it and he..." Miss Crauford hesitated and took a deep breath. "He has not."

"Give him time," Temperance soothed. "It is a scary thought to give into something so intangible. I fear that he is only trying to protect himself from the terror that was our parent's union." Temperance visible shuddered and Teresa frowned. "With patience, I think Isaac will find a way to open his heart to love," Temperance continued. "It is a strange thing and yet wonderful." She smiled at her friend trying to give her hope.

"And what of your heart?" Teresa asked with keen observation.

"We are not speaking of me," Temperance deflected. "I have no interest in marriage." Though, even to her own ears, for the first time, her words fell flat and she felt as though she had spoken falsely. She shook her head to strengthen her resolve. "I shall never marry." The truth was she knew she could not. She was ruined. She could not foist herself upon someone she loved with a lie. Not now that she had seen what love looked like; felt like. Her heart could not bear it.

WHEN THE CARRIAGES BEGAN TO ARRIVE FOR THE BALL, Temperance could hardly keep her eyes from staring. The neighborhood was filled with some of the most prominent families in England. Without the hustle and bustle of the city, they had surrounded themselves with friends and beauty. Their wealth and prestige were apparent. Temperance's ball gown, a voluminous creation of satin folds in a brilliant emerald green, had seemed just the color for the jewel-toned season. Compared to the intricate embellishments and brocades of the incoming gowns, she felt the simplicity of her shimmering fabric might appear plain. However, one thing she had in her favor was the effect of Miss Merton's abundant skill.

The dress fit her like a glove. The bodice was tight beneath her breasts, and hugged her trim waist with the slight flare of the skirt so that she appeared both petite and curvaceous at the same time. The wide cut of the neckline, nearly off the shoulders, set her small bust to look ample enough without being buxom or indecent. Her mother had offered one small teardrop pearl to hang from a silver chain as thin as a spider's silk. The understated elegance made her abashed at first, but the nod of approval from her brother and the poignant regard of Evan Crauford's eyes told her that she had done well for herself.

Teresa wore an ivory gown with a matching lace overlay and the softest slippers that Temperance had ever touched. The entire outfit had been a gift for her eighteenth birthday and, though she had worn it previously, it was still her favorite. She shrugged as she thought of others who would only wear a gown once. "I like it," she said. "And I shall wear it."

Temperance admired her spirit.

The ladies entered the ballroom with their arms linked and their chins held high. Their brothers followed at a respectable distance, giving a scolding eye to any gentleman who looked too long upon their sisters.

The music began and the Lord and Lady Pepperton opened the ball with a flourish.

"You know that my mother could not dance a lick before she married father," Teresa giggled. "She said that she had spent too many years upon her pianoforte bench and never quite learned how to stand upon her feet. She had always been a bit shy, and what with the mark upon her face, and she had never properly learned. My grandfather thought no one would ever dance with her, but Father did. In time, he taught her all the steps. She said that they would spend entire evenings dancing alone to nothing more than the tinkling of a music box." She smiled at Temperance, and Temperance remembered the first night that she had enlisted Teresa's help to learn dance steps. "I still have the music box," Teresa admitted.

"She dances beautifully," Temperance observed. She watched the pair gaze lovingly into one another's eyes. If the Viscount Pepperton noticed any flaw in his wife, there was no sign of it. If anything, he appeared to think her more beautiful for her unique coloring.

The pair gave a gesture and their children joined in the opening set, followed closely by Temperance and her brother. Isaac was also a skilled dancer, Temperance observed. He must have learned such grace outside of their home because, though the siblings had played at dancing with one another, there had been little chance for other partners with which to practice. The Lord and Lady Mortel had never danced together, at least, not in all of Temperance's recollection. She supposed they must have when they were courting, but she could not picture it.

As soon as the set ended, Temperance was surprised to find a line of gentlemen awaiting her hand. She allowed herself to be passed from one to the other until there was no way that she could recall all of their names. They were all kind and amusing in their own ways. Compliments were paid to her beauty, but in such a way as prevented her from feeling like a piece of bait that had been laid for a fox-hunt.

Perhaps, she thought, this is how the higher echelon of society was meant to behave. Her own experiences, surrounded by her father's grotesque acquaintances, may not have been the norm. The realization hit her like a stone to the head, or the heart more like. The thought filled her with a buoyancy that she had never experienced. After passing comments about her beauty, the conversation in her own home had always lagged. However, there was something about this space that seemed above indiscretion and inappropriate advances. She had no fear and therefore gave herself over to enjoying the evening.

Before she knew it, several hours had passed and Temperance had yet to leave the floor. She begged her leave from the next dance and made her way over to a large table that was peppered with a varied selection of refreshments. It was a bold decision when she accepted a flute of wine. She rarely imbibed in the drink because she had heard tell that it might be used to weaken the will of a lady when she might otherwise be resolute. Still, the cool refreshment rejuvenated her energy and cooled the flush of her skin. When she turned, a hand waving in the air caught her attention. Miss Crauford was calling her over from a short distance away where she stood flanked by her own family and Temperance's brother.

"Has tonight not been a dream?" Teresa asked once her friend had joined them.

"I have never had a better time in my entire life," Temperance admitted and offered her compliments to the Viscountess. Lady Pepperton thanked Temperance and begged that she come again, and often.

"It seems many of our young men are quite taken with our newcomer," she said with a smile.

Temperance felt a blush rise in her cheeks. She cared not for the attention but could finally say that she understood how some ladies were able to enjoy such company. She understood the appeal of an evening dancing and holding conversation with strangers as she never had before.

"Whispers are calling you the most beautiful lady in the room." Lady Pepperton continued. "Even Miss Pentington is sour about it," she said with a look towards Mr. Crauford who just joined them.

"Oh I never meant to make anyone sour," Temperance said with concern, glancing from Lady Pepperton to her son.

"Mother, Temperance is too shy for such compliments," Teresa laughed.

"Not at all my dear," Lady Pepperton laughed with the same lighthearted grin as her daughter.

"Clarice Pentington is sour whenever she is not the

center of attention," Mr. Crauford said. "She is not used to being upstaged."

"Besides which, she is cross because you have been avoiding her all evening. Isn't that so, Evan?"

"Mother," Mr. Crauford said with a cross scowl.

"Well, even if you are too much a gentleman to admit it," his sister replied, "we can all see that you have kept to the opposite side of room all evening. I've watched you both like a game of chess. It is most amusing. She crosses the floor, and before she can set upon you, you've hurried away."

Mr. Crauford seemed not a bit amused.

His family laughed at his misfortune and went on to explain that the aforementioned Miss Pentington had been in pursuit of Evan for as long as they could all remember.

"Well, I suppose I should avoid checkmate as long as I am able," Mr. Crauford commented grimly.

The laughter began anew.

Temperance found the gentleman's discomfort endearing. Despite his obvious disinterest in the lady, he wished to avoid a blatant affront or harm to her feelings.

He said he had hoped that he had done better to hide his avoidance so as not to bring about upset or whispers.

"You have yet to ask me to dance," Teresa confronted the Viscount Mortel with one quirked eyebrow.

Isaac laughed at her bold proposition and teased that he was waiting for a set that was up to her skill. She called him a scoundrel and pretended to be offended. "Perhaps the last dance," Isaac suggested and Teresa with stars in her eyes accepted.

Temperance sipped her wine and allowed the drink to warm her, a pleasant sensation that she had never expected to enjoy.

"Why, Evan!" a deep, romantic voice filled with femininity crooned from behind Temperance. The startled reaction of the group was so sudden that Temperance nearly spit her drink in a most ill-mannered way. Instead, Temperance was forced to turn aside in a fit of unladylike coughing. "What a shame that our paths have not crossed earlier in the evening." Miss Pentington offered her greetings to the Lord and Lady Pepperton as the host and hostess and gave a quick nod to the Baggington siblings to whom she waited to be introduced.

Evan did the honors and the lady's gaze turned at once to Temperance, who had at this point recovered. With shrewd eyes the lady looked Temperance over. Temperance did her best not to squirm under the inspection, but it was clear that she was being leveled with the attempt to determine whether or not she might be a threat to Miss Pentington's designs upon Mr. Crauford.

There was nothing the matter with Miss Pentington, Temperance determined. She had fine features, cool blue eyes, and pretty golden hair that Temperance had admired from afar earlier in the evening. Her dress was fine but not at all revealing or overdone in its style. Temperance realized that she might have liked her well enough, had she not been warned of the lady's uncomfortable persistence toward Mr. Crauford.

"The Master of Ceremonies just announced the last

set," Miss Pentington whined and waited for her hint to be received. "Though, I do wish that the ball could go on for always."

"What a shame that it must be over," Lord Pepperton intoned with no help to his son. His smile was tucked in such a way that it was clear that he was well amused by the younger man's predicament. He offered his hand to his wife and gave a low bow. "Come, my lady," he grinned, "we shall finish our evening as it began."

Miss Pentington waited impatiently for an offer that was unforthcoming. Mr. Crauford opened his mouth, unable to refuse the lady without causing a slight. Temperance, recalling his rescue of her from Lord Vardemere, spoke before he could make the offer.

"Oh dear, if the Master has called the last set, then we had best be off," she said to the group. "Mr. Crauford and I did agree upon a dance, so I suppose we must fulfill the promise now or shall be shamed to have not kept our word."

Miss Pentington's mouth fell open in tandem to Mr. Crauford's expanding smile. Dark eyes twinkling he offered his arm to Temperance.

"If you would excuse us," he gave a respectable nod to Miss Pentington, before turning to Isaac and Teresa. "Come along, you two. It seems we have less time than we thought."

Teresa took Isaac's arm and together the couples left the aggressive young lady standing in defeat.

18

"You are full of surprises Miss. Baggington," Mr. Crauford whispered as he pulled Temperance against him for the waltz.

"You end a ball on a waltz?" Temperance asked suddenly feeling self-conscious. This was the one dance that she and Teresa had not been able to practice. Besides, her comment to Mr. Crauford was now considered much more forward than she had known. He did not seem to mind. His eyes were shining as he spoke.

"It is mother and father's favorite," he explained. "They say that they prefer to end the evening on a romantic note."

"Oh," Temperance mouthed the word but no sound came forth. She felt a blush heat her face. Mr. Crauford must think her extremely forward to have placed herself in his arms for the waltz. At the mention of romance, she felt feverish. The ruse of dancing had merely been an offer of salvation to her friend. She had not quite thought through what it might require. Of course, she had danced with Mr. Crauford once before, but something about that had been different. Perhaps she had not known him so well that first time, or perhaps she liked him better now? Perhaps it was the wine, she wondered, but knew that it could not be because she had disposed of the half-filled glass before they had entered the dance floor.

Her heart fluttered in her chest. She wondered if he could feel it pulsing through her body with the hand that was braced against her lower back. If he could, he gave no sign of it.

"You could have danced with her," Temperance blurted. "I only thought..."

"Oh, I much prefer this," Mr Crauford said with a graveling tone that set her heart beating fast. He shifted her a hair closer, closer than Temperance had ever danced with a gentleman before. Or, at least, it felt closer. It felt as if she could feel the heat from beneath his coat flowing toward her. The room felt small around them, and her head spun faster than their twirling about the floor. She was going to misstep, she was sure of it.

"We can stop, if you'd like," he offered noticing her discomfort. Though he had sounded loathe to say the words, the offer meant a great deal to her. Still, Temperance felt terrible that he had taken her words to mean that she had not wished to partner him. She leaned more fully against him, telling herself that it was for the ease of the dance, and smiled in return. She felt giddy with excitement.

"I much prefer this," she said with a shy whisper. "Only I am not so skilled a dancer." She turned her face away so that he might not see her blush and she could not see his reaction. "I apologize if I trod on your toes."

"You are light as a feather, Miss Baggington. I shall not be hurt by a misstep, although I must say, I have seen no fault thus far."

Temperance felt giddy at his praise. She had never felt this type of nervous excitement around a gentleman. Certainly she had felt nervous, or afraid, but never before, would she have called the sensation pleasurable. There was something nice about the feeling in this moment, just as there had been in the music room. A mixture of the fluttering in her stomach and racing of her heart made her feel as though her insides had been turned to liquid heat. She wondered if Evan might feel the same. His sister had told tales of the ladies who had tried to catch his interest, but he had yet to fall in love with any of them. Would it be possible that he might fall in love with her?

Love? She would not dare to think that was what she was feeling. However, Temperance began to wonder if she was in the beginnings of it. Could it be that she was falling in love with Mr. Evan Crauford? To think that only a few months ago she had been sitting in the isolated rooms of an abbey with no thought to marriage or love of any sort. It seemed a dream. She shook her head to rid her mind of the thought. It could not be. She was damaged goods. Even if she wanted Evan, for her own... Evan she thought, letting his Christian name settle in her thoughts. Even if she wanted him as her husband, she must let him go.

The song ended and with trembling lips she thanked

him for the pleasure. Then, before he could speak she turned upon her heal and rushed away. From the corner of her eye she saw Miss Pentington detain him from the attempt to follow. Temperance was too flustered to deal with any more emotions this evening. Rather, she looked for Teresa and discovered that she and her brother Isaac had finished the dance and were still standing in each other's arms with eyes for only each other, as were Lord and Lady Pepperton. Temperance thought she must find a moment away, and so she fled out the doors to the garden. The icy rain did not fall on the veranda, but it was still bitter outside. She immediately began to rethink her choice of venue and turned to reenter the ballroom, but Mr. Crauford who seemed to have rid himself of Miss Pentington stood in the doorway in all his glory. He was utterly perfect, she told herself, and she could not have him. She did not move. She only stood with eyes wide as if she had been caught at some naughtiness.

"Why did you flee?" he asked. "Did I offend you in some way?"

"No, of course not," she answered hastily. "I only thought, the dance had ended and..." She let her voice trail off as she suppressed a shiver. He stepped closer to her, unbuttoning his jacket. He took it off and wrapped the garment around her shoulders before she could protest. She was inundated in his scent. She breathed it in thinking if she never had another moment with him, this must be enough. She was in love with him, she realized, but nothing could come of the revelation. She was tainted, and he was a true gentleman.

He took her hand loose from where she clenched his jacket close, and wrapped her in his arms.

"You must be cold," she said looking at the expanse of his shirt and waistcoat over his chest.

"Hardly," he said with a hint of mirth. She could feel the length of him and the heat of him. Somehow, here in the darkness it was a more intimate moment than she had ever experienced. She did not move from his arms although she knew she should. Then he whispered his breath against her ear. "I want to kiss you, Miss Baggington."

She wanted that too, with all her heart, but she shook her head. "You mustn't," she said.

"Very well." He took a breath, and stepped back, still holding her hands. She did not pull away from him.

"Isaac said that you possess a delicate sensibility, and..." he hesitated. "I have known Isaac for a long time You know that," he confessed. "I consider us like brothers. You must know I value his friendship... and yours."

Friendship? Was that what this was? She did not think friendship truly described the giddy feeling within her breast, but she did not contradict him. "I know Isaac values your friendship," she said.

"I don't want to speak of Isaac," he said shaking his head. "I want to speak of us."

Us, Temperance thought. "There cannot be an us," she whispered. "I can't..."

"You must know how much I admire you," he interrupted.

"And I you, but ..."

The silence stretched between them and Temperance did not know what to say. She knew she should pull away. She should go inside, but she could not bring herself to take his hands from hers. He had begun to rub a circle at her wrist where the end of her glove allowed his touch. "I should go," she said at last and he stilled his hand.

"Do you wish to?" He asked.

"I must."

"I have feelings for you, Miss Baggington. I am sure you have noticed and I hope you might have feelings for me. Only tell me true."

She shook her head, but could not quite deny him verbally.

"Is it not so?"

She shook her head, but did not speak.

He sighed. "Teresa thought..." he stopped and bit his lip. Temperance waited for him to finish, but he said nothing.

"What?" she asked. What had Teresa said of her?

"My sister is an observant woman. Teresa only suggested that you might have been hurt in the past. She suggested that you might be hesitant to trust...a gentleman with ...your heart, and I should be patient. I am trying to be patient," he said. "I am trying, but I am finding it very difficult." He released her hands, and stepped away. "I know that your father was not a loving man, but..."

Temperance snorted: a most unladylike sound. Still she did not want to speak of her father, but she remained silent allowing Mr. Crauford to finish.

"I understand you have no example of a loving

household," Mr. Crauford continued as he paced. "I know this from Isaac, and to hear tell from him, your father did seem to be a difficult man," he said. "Although he surely cannot be as bad as Isaac paints him."

"I assure you he was far worse," she whispered, and then covered her lips. Surely she should not say so.

He looked at her sharply.

She saw when the realization crossed his face, horror, disbelief and then pity all flashed forth, and in the next moment, he reached out to her saying her Christian name for the first time. "Oh, Temperance…"

He caught her arm and drew her close so that she could see the hurt in his eyes, hurt for her and for what could never be.

"I love you," he said, but the words could not be. He could not love her. Not as she was. She pulled away panic filling her.

"Let me go," she demanded and he released her. She spoke, then, trying to explain and keep some measure of dignity. "We Baggingtons have more skeletons in our closets than we would care to count, and if you knew the truth of them you would not only refuse association with me, but you should forbid Teresa my brother as well."

"No. I would never. You are your own person, Miss Baggington, as is Isaac. I am not so shallow as to let a few skeletons frighten me. I love you," he said more seriously now, as if he were sure of himself, "And I think you have feelings for me as well, I want to court you. I want you in my life, if you would have me."

She stood shaking her head no. At last she made the

words come from her mouth. "No," she said. "I cannot. You cannot...You cannot love me."

He drew himself up a little in front of her. "You may say what *you* cannot do, Miss Baggington, but you cannot say what *I feel*, and I know without a doubt I am in love with you. What came before does not matter."

She shook her head in denial. She was damaged. How could he not see that?

"Can you not recognize your own feelings? Look at me and tell me your do not love me." He pulled her close and she looked into his dark eyes; so intense in this moment. She knew she could not say the word for it was true. She did love him. She could not look him in the eye and speak falsely.

"I cannot," she said her voice dropping to a whisper. "I do love you, but it cannot be." She looked away in shame.

He tilted her chin up so that she had to look at him again. "If there is love, that is all that matters," he said. "I want to bring the music back into your life, Miss Baggington. Please, allow me to try."

She shook her head. "I cannot be the lady you deserve," she said, the tears falling freely now. Her voice drop to a barely audible whisper. "I am... ruined, and I will not be a party to a relationship based on falsehood."

"You are the only woman I want," he said. "There is no falsehood in you. I see you for who you are, and I have been in love with your since the first day I met you. The day you returned home with full of hope for a better tomorrow. I want nothing more than to love and protect you for the rest of my life. Nothing you can say will make me not want you." He caught her hand again and caressed it. "I understand that you are frightened, but please, allow me to prove my sincerity. I will not disappoint you; I promise this."

"I believe you," she said at last, but her feelings were so turbulent, she could not make sense of them. She had to flee. "Good night, Mr. Crauford," she whispered hastily and hurried back inside. It was not until the heat of the fire hit her that she realized she still wore Mr. Crauford's coat. She took it off and held it for a moment more, breathing in the scent of him before she laid it over a chair. Then she hurried to her room. She did not want to speak with her brother or Teresa just now. She wanted to hold all her feelings close until she could sort them. For the first time in her life, she felt the light of happiness shining upon her. Mr. Crauford loved her. Was it possible that he loved her regardless of her past?

19

---

*T*he Baggingtons remained at Pepperton Hill for another six days. In that time, Temperance was left to observe her gentleman of interest with great care. Isaac and Teresa, whether or not they cared to admit it, were prone to arranging time for themselves alone. This left Temperance to Evan's company, which she found that she enjoyed. He did not push her for an answer. Neither spoke of their heated conversation in the garden, but he did sit beside her on the bench as they played music together.

Every day they grew closer and closer and, though Temperance changed the topic whenever Mr. Crauford seemed to lead the conversation toward their feelings, she felt that he could sense that she was growing fonder of him by the hour. He did not grow frustrated with her shy approach. He was patient and kind. Temperance found that her favorite pastime was making music together, followed closely by trips to the lake shore. They would watch Isaac and Teresa in their fishing competition, which was a near daily activity as long as the weather held. Temperance would curl up amongst the blankets and pillows with Evan near enough, but not touching. There was an intimacy about it that brought a thrill to her heart. Now, she understood why their siblings preferred activities where they could manage to find their isolation without entering a situation that would raise question. If they were happened upon, the pairs could simply say that they were passing their leisure in the company of friends.

When it came time to say their farewells, it was with a heavy heart. Temperance hated to think about leaving the serenity and beauty of Pepperton Hill. Not only was the home magnificent, but it housed her most dear friend as well as the gentleman that she had come to love.

As their carriage rounded the bend to settle in front of the steps to Mortel Manor, Temperance and Isaac were both lost in their own thoughts. She wondered if her brother too was missing someone that he had left behind. Mortel Manor seemed cold in comparison to the light and joy at Pepperton Hill.

Nearly a week passed and Temperance was missing Mr. Crauford more than she expected. As she came down to breakfast on the sixth day, the twins were waiting at the landing of the stairs with a level of excitement that was startling.

"Oh you must come see!" they cried as soon as Temperance made her descent.

"It arrived just this morning" Hope said in a tumbling burst of words.

"I've never seen anything so beautiful," Faith continued at a similar pace. "We are just dying to know who it is from. We haven't opened the letter although I cannot deny that we had discussed attempting a peek."

Isaac pinched the arch of his nose between two fingers as he begged his sisters to slow down and tell them what all of the fuss was about.

"Come look," Hope hopped toward the door and begged that they follow her.

Temperance and Isaac did so. In the middle of the hall they were told to close their eyes and be led by their hands to the item that had caused such a stir. Temperance could hardly contain her curiosity but every time that she attempted to peer through the squint in her eyes she was harshly reprimanded.

Eventually, the pair was brought to a halt and commanded to open their eyes.

They were standing in the middle of the empty music hall, except that it was no longer empty. In the center of the room stood the immense form of a curved pianoforte.

Temperance stood in shocked silence for the longest moment until Isaac instructed her to open the note that had come with it. Neither of them had need to check the name. It could only have been sent to her by Evan Crauford.

Her heart beat in her chest as she peeled the wax seal from the envelope. Her hands trembled and tears of joy welled in her eyes as she read.

This shall need to suffice until your return to Pepperton Hill. Please enjoy, though, do not become overly fond for it is meant to stay as the first installment of the Lord Mortel's new collection.

I hope that I might bring the music back to your life.

Teresa sends her love.

E.

"Well?" the twins asked in unison.

"It's for Isaac," Temperance stumbled over the words.

"Oh, don't be daft," Isaac grabbed at the letter to read for himself but Temperance clutched it to her chest and would not allow it. "It's obvious that it is meant for you, sister." He finished lamely.

"It is the first addition to your replacement of the music hall," Temperance assured him with a grin that she could not contain. It was the truth, after all. Though there was much more to unpack in the letter which she refused to share with her siblings.

Evan had sent the pianoforte *to suffice until her return* and said specifically *not to grow attached.* Why would he say such a thing if he did not intend her to leave it behind at some point in the future? He could not, she wondered with a thrill, be referencing the potential that she might one day come to Pepperton Hill, and that music hall, on a more permanent basis? *I hope that I might bring the music back to your life.* He had, she thought, with his person alone.

"Who is it from?" Hope begged.

"Evan Crauford," Isaac said with a knowing shrug.

Temperance nodded. "What a kind gesture from your friend," she replied. Then, under the pressure of her brother's exaggerated stare, she could not help breaking in to a fit of laughter.

"Alright, it is for my pleasure too," she admitted, "for now."

Her eyes locked with her brother and she nodded.

"Then I approve," he said.

Again, she nodded.

The unspoken words hung between them. Temperance would return Pepperton Hill.

"I do not understand," Faith pouted.

"That's alright, little one," Isaac said as he flung an arm across her shoulder. "You have no need to comprehend such things yet."

The twins huffed but could get no more information from their elder siblings.

Temperance sat to the instrument and began to play. She poured her heart into the music, into her love for the gentleman who had gifted it to her. She would play every day until she saw him and could thank him properly. Until then, she would hone her craft so that she could play well when she saw him once again. Indeed he did bring the music back into her life, the music that her father had broken. But she herself was not broken she decided as her heart began to sing.

Her cheeks grew red with the thought of her thanks. She would kiss him, she decided. She had many weeks until they crossed paths again to work up the courage, but she would kiss him. Boldly and unafraid. Then, she would spill her heart at his feet and beg him to take her as she was. He would accept her, of that she now had no doubt. He would love her as if she had never known a hardship in her life. He, like his father had his mother, would look beyond her flaws and see the beauty within.

Temperance cried as she plucked at the keys with her trembling fingers. For the first time she cried with joy. She cried with love. Most of all, she cried with happiness at the thought of her future and all of the promise that it held.

Temperance had decided that she would accept Mr. Crauford as he accepted her, unconditionally.

EPILOGUE

*S*everal weeks had passed and it was with mixed feelings that she next spoke to Teresa. Temperance and her brother Isaac had been again invited to Pepperton Hall. Temperance was under the impression that Isaac had edged his way into the invitation which embarrassed Temperance, but her brother was adamant.

"Do not have a care, sister. All will be well. We are welcome."

It was with some trepidation on Temperance's part that she and her brother Isaac arrived the evening before, and she found her eyes drawn to Evan. He was so very handsome. She wished that they could have but a moment alone. How else could she give him his kiss of thanksgiving? The thought made the color rise in her cheeks.

They made small talk around the supper table but there was no time for privacy, so Temperance was surprised to learn that somehow Isaac found that sought after moment alone. Teresa bubbled into the breakfast room with Isaac in her wake. "We are engaged," she announced to the siblings seated at the breakfast table. "Isaac asked me to marry him."

"And Miss Crauford made me the happiest man in the world when she said yes," Isaac added with a hand on the small of her back.

Temperance stood to embrace her friend, and whispered in her ear, "When? When did he ask you?"

"You are not the only one who enjoys midnight dancing," Teresa replied with no sign of shame or embarrassment. Teresa hugged her tighter.

"Now, we will truly be sisters," Temperance said. She could not help but throw a glance towards Evan, but for once he was not looking at her. He was deep in conversation with Isaac.

"And I shall truly be a Baggington," Teresa said. Temperance could not help but be happy for her and for Isaac.

She looked at Mr. Crauford. He seemed very quiet and Temperance was afraid that he would not propose at all, and yet did they not have an accord? She was sure of it, but comparing what feeling was between her and Mr. Crauford to the mad love affair of his parents, she could understand his hesitancy. How could he accept her so readily, when she was indeed damaged goods? Perhaps he had reconsidered. Temperance had convinced herself that despite the extravagance of his gift he could not want to marry her, when he invited her into the music room.

"Which is your favorite?" Mr. Crauford asked.

"The harp," she said without hesitation.

"Ah," Mr. Crauford said. "The choice of an angel."

Temperance blushed prettily as Mr. Crauford gestured for her to sit at the harp. She sat and brushed her fingers over the instrument. As she began to play, Mr. Crauford joined her. She stopped. "Don't stop," he encouraged her and she began again. As they played, Temperance realized that they were in perfect harmony. At last they completed the piece, and Temperance looked down. She did not realize that Mr. Crauford had moved closer to her and brought her to her feet. "I want to make beautiful music with you, Miss Baggington. I want you in my life forever. I know you have some reservations with men, but I hope you will allow me to prove the trustworthiness of my gender."

She nodded, uncertain what to say. Was he proposing?

"May I kiss you?" he asked.

She nodded unable to quite speak and his lips descended upon hers. He had claimed that she was an angel, but it was his kiss that transported her to heaven. She opened her eyes. He was but a breath away from her. "Marry me, Miss Baggington." he said. "Be my wife."

"Yes!" she said and he kissed her again, deepening the kiss until she felt a fiery heat flowing through her.

She knew such kisses were not to be shared between unmarried couples, but she did not want to ever let him go. She clung to him like he was life itself until the noise of someone clearing their throat made her pull away.

There, standing in the doorway to the music room

stood her brother and Teresa. Teresa clapped and said excitedly, "Now we will be sisters twice over."

"About time," Isaac said punched Evan playfully. "Good on you," he said.

"It took you months to work up the nerve to ask my sister," Evan retorted.

"How long?" Temperance asked breathlessly. "How long have you been standing there?"

"Since the chorus," Teresa said gleefully as the two couples walked back towards the drawing room. "We saw the whole thing."

Temperance blushed red thinking of the passion of their kiss.

"Do not worry," Isaac said. "We shan't tell about your kiss if you do not tell about our midnight dancing."

"Isaac!" Evan admonished. "Midnight dancing! That's my sister. Shall I have to call you out?" He teased.

"She is soon to be my wife," Isaac said as Evan called for a bottle of wine to celebrate. Glasses were poured all around and they toasted each other's happiness, while Isaac decried the lack of Champagne due to the war in France.

"Hopefully those brothers of yours will soon return home," Evan said.

"Perhaps in time for the wedding," Isaac added.

"Weddings." Evan corrected as he put a hand on the small of Temperance's back. The touch did not frighten her. On the contrary, she felt loved and protected. She turned her head up to him and he kissed her. "I think we shall play together each evening just as my parents ride," Evan said. "What do you think, Miss Baggington?"

"I think it is a marvelous idea." She looked at her brother and Teresa. "And what about you," Temperance asked. "What will be your special time together?"

"Fishing!" Teresa proclaimed and Temperance and Evan broke into laughter. Eventually, Isaac joined in, but whispered to Teresa, "In the winter, it shall be midnight dancing." Teresa smiled up at him, and Temperance saw the love in their stare. Temperance turned to her own Mr. Crauford who was smiling back at her. She lost herself to his gaze, knowing her own eyes reflected the same depth of feeling. She never wanted this moment to end and realized with a start that it didn't have too. Love is forever, she thought and she allowed Evan to draw her into his embrace.

CONTINUE READING FOR A SNEAK PEEK OF...

The Healing Heart ~ Mercy
by Isabella Thorne

1

_M_ercy was not well-trained in the female art of conversation. Her father had preferred her silent and biddable. Now she found herself ill-equipped for polite conversation, both from her own introversion and from the general isolation in which the Baggington daughters had been raised. Mercy felt more inclined to sit in a pleasurable silence than boisterous chatter. Once again, she thought that Simon ought to have brought the twins. They were lively and talkative. Perhaps they might be better at finding a common ground with General Bradley.

"You are going to worry your lip right off if you do not stop," Simon teased as they bumped along the road. Mercy realized that she had been nibbling her lower lip and ceased the offensive action at once. "You get on just fine with me," her brother said in a soothing tone, "Edmund is not so different."

"I thought that you said he was quite outgoing," she recalled.

"He was," Simon nodded, "and he will be again. For now, however, he is just getting back into the swing of things."

Mercy wondered what he meant by such a statement and when she asked, Simon only muttered something about how she would see soon enough. A moment later they pulled up in front of the house. Mercy thought it beautiful, even though the intermittent rain and snow had left its mark. She could see where there would be a pleasant little vegetable garden off to the side and there was even a pen around the back where animals might be kept. She thought she heard the clucking of hens, but could not say for certain. It would have been rude to explore the grounds before knocking on the door and making their introduction.

The painted white door was opened to reveal the happiest grin that Mercy had seen in ages.

"Mr. Baggington!" the old woman cried and ushered the siblings inside before the threat of rain might begin to fall. "What a pleasure! And who might this be?" she offered a wink, "Your beautiful wife?"

"No," Simon laughed. "Mrs. Smith, I would like you to meet my sister, Miss Mercy Baggington."

Mrs. Smith clucked her tongue, not unlike the chickens out of doors, as if she thought Simon ought to be wed by now. Still, she turned to Mercy with a welcome smile and declared her a breath of fresh air in this world of men.

Mercy soon learned that Mrs. Anne Smith was General Bradley's housekeeper though Mercy suspected that her role was more as a mothering figure than anything else. She did seem quite affectionate and spoke nothing but praise of the man.

"Call me Annie, please," the woman begged. "You'll meet my husband if you are ever about the grounds and neither of us care to stand on formality. Annie and Barry will do just fine. Now, follow me, the General is just in from the stables, and I am sure he could use a bit of cheering up. Mornings have been cross around here, as you well know, Mr. Baggington."

Mercy felt slightly alarmed that they might be stepping in upon a cross gentleman. Her father being cross had meant that all of his children were like to make themselves scarce in order to prevent falling prey to one of his violent rages. Cross might mean that the General did not want visitors. When she said as much, Simon shook his head and followed Mrs. Smith. Mercy had nothing else to do but trudge along behind, all the while wondering if they ought to have come at all.

The sitting room was well lit as it was positioned in such a way that allowed for a roaring fire on one wall and two full opposing walls covered with windows. It was pleasant and inviting. Mercy felt at once at home.

"General Bradley," the housekeeper announced. "You have guests."

Mercy bristled as she saw movement on the far side of the room. From her vantage point she could see the back of a tall wing-backed chair in front of the fire. The figure behind it made a slow effort to rise. She anticipated being met with a scowl or glare, but the General's face seemed at first filled with determined concentration. Then, once he looked up, it broke into an uneven grin as he greeted his friend and waved them into the room.

At first Mercy had not noticed his use of a cane. At least, not until he rounded the chair with some difficulty.

"I apologize," General Bradley laughed in a self-depreciating manner, "I am a bit sore and slow moving this morning."

"Still no success?" Simon asked. He moved further into the room so that the General might not have to move so far.

"No," the General shook his head. "I have landed on my ..." He paused with the sight of Mercy, and rephrased for her feminine ears. "I have been unseated more times than I care to count. At this point, I am not sure that it is worth attempting any further. Perhaps my physician is right after all. I should just sit in my chair and thank my stars I am alive at all."

"Nonsense," Simon waved away the comment. "It is for that reason that I have brought my sister."

Mercy's eyes opened wide as her brother gestured her way. She had no idea what he was talking about and from the look upon his face he was well aware that she would have declined if he had given her any advance information as to what he was up to. It seemed that this was to be more than just a single amicable visit. She threw Simon a look that would have withered him when he was younger, but he only grinned back at her. Mercy remembered her manners and smiled at the General regardless to her ire at her brother.

Introductions were made and the General offered the siblings seats by the fire. Simon chose a second wingback chair and Mercy seated herself on a covered stool at her brother's side. Both she and General Bradley eagerly waited for Simon's explanation.

"Mercy is an avid rider," he said finally, and Mercy raised an eyebrow. Whatever was Simon on about?

"She is the most skilled I have ever seen, even more than any man," Simon explained.

If he thought flattery was going to soften her towards him he was wrong, Mercy thought as he continued.

"If there is anyone who can help you learn to ride again it would be she."

Mercy shook her head. "I have never given lessons," she protested. "Really, Simon, this is not my skill. I only ride for my own pleasure."

"Edmund knows how to ride," Simon replied. "He just needs to figure out a way to manage with a leg on only one side of the horse."

Mercy was confused and her expression must have revealed as much. With a sigh, General Bradley pulled up the leg of his trouser to reveal a false limb. Having been attached to a shoe at the base, it had gone quite unnoticed by Mercy in the few moments that the gentleman had been standing. Now she understood why it was that he used a cane. She had known he was injured for he was far too young to need the use of a cane for any other purpose, but she had not known he was missing his leg. She estimated that he was perhaps a decade older than herself, but found that he still had a youthfulness about him. It was no wonder that he had developed a friendship with her younger brothers.

In fact, she thought with a blush, he was quite attractive. Had he not been missing a limb, Mercy would assume that he would have had flocks of ladies swarming for his attention. She shook such thoughts from her mind. It did not matter whether or not the gentleman was attractive, even though he was, she had no knowledge of how to teach a man with one leg to ride, and Simon had no right to assume that she would do so. She threw her brother another scowl behind the General's notice.

General Bradley seemed to have the keen ability to sense her hesitation.

"It is only off just above the knee," he explained with an embarrassed grimace. "That's the rub. If I could have kept it to below, I think I would have it. I just can't seem to hang on."

"I am sorry for your plight, truly," she explained and then turned to her brother. "But I do not see how I can be of service."

"We have got to be missing something," Simon said.

"Yes," General Bradley laughed, "my leg!"

Mercy had been steeled in her refusal until the moment of the General's comment. At his words her mouth dropped open in shock and it took everything in her power not to laugh. It would have been rude, except that he had been the one to make the joke, so as she looked upon his chuckling form she could not help herself. Both the gentlemen were laughing. Mercy succumbed to soft hiccups which made them both laugh even harder when she could not stop.

"Oh dear," she covered her mouth with her hand, and the General, with some curtesy called for Mrs. Smith to bring her a drink of water. Once Mercy had her breath again, Simon persisted in his urging.

"Give it a go, Mercy," Simon begged. "If you fail we are no worse off than before... but if you succeed, it would be a miracle."

"I would give anything to sit a horse again without making a fool of myself," General Bradley explained. "If I could sit a horse they might even give me my command again."

"General..." Simon began.

"Is that what you want?" Mercy asked unaccustomedly interrupting Simon. It seemed to her that if she had been so grievously injured in battle on horseback, the back of a horse would be the last place that she would wish to return.

"The war is over," the General shrugged, "at least it is for me. I have no intention of returning to the field to fight, but it would be something to be able to consult on tactics now and then. To do so, I would need to be able to make the ride to the regiment camps and then back out again. You can't take a carriage to war."

Mercy nodded. That made sense. Still, if the gentleman had been attempting to ride already and had been unable to hold his seat, she was not certain that she could be of any service.

"What if you injure yourself further?" she asked. Did he not see that this dream was reckless? Would it not be safer to just live out his days in the comfort of his home surrounded by friends? Why would he want to, quite literally, get back on the horse?

The General's brow furrowed as if to say that the answer was obvious.

"Is the possibility of injury worth giving up the chance to ride again?" he asked. "You say you are an avid rider, Miss Baggington. Would you give it up forever?" He paused. "Even if I only ride for pleasure, is that not worth the risk?"

Mercy could not imagine what her life would be without the freedom that she felt when she raced through the fields upon her faithful steed. To be denied even that small freedom would have broken her, especially if she had lost a limb. She could see that same look in General Bradley's eyes. He may be able to walk and move about, but he had lost the freedom of speed. Indeed, he had been bound to the ground for far too long, feeling trapped by his infirmity, and the inability to control his body as he wished. She understood feeling trapped.

"Very well," she said with a nod. "I shall try. When do we begin?"

"Not until tomorrow," the General laughed and groaned at the same time. "I think that I have spent my chances for this day. That is," he amended, "if you do not have prior commitments."

"I never have commitments," Mercy said breezily before she could stop herself. She was mortified and stammered to clarify her response. "What I mean is that I do not have any commitments that cannot be adjusted."

Both gentlemen allowed her blunder to slip by without comment, but she could see that they were amused. Simon, of course, knew that Mercy had no gentlemen callers with prior engagements. That did not mean that she needed to go parading that knowledge around to anyone who asked. She chastised herself for her lack of social prowess. Of course she would make a fool of herself straight away.

"We shall begin tomorrow," the General confirmed. "Until then, would you care for some tea?"

Mercy wanted nothing more than to return home and resume the visit tomorrow. Tea meant she would have to talk to the gentleman, but it seemed that Simon was true to his word in holding the conversation. Mercy remained silent, lost in her own thoughts, as the men shared tales of their daring adventures. She could see now that Simon had tricked her into not one, but potentially many, future visits on behalf of his friend. How long might it take them to be successful in the attempt?

There was one thing that she was thankful for, that Simon was not attempting to secure any sort of romantic match between the pair as she had first suspected. Her brother was well aware of her thoughts and feelings on the matter although the subject of why she felt this way, was scrupulously avoided.

Furthermore, Simon had written to her of the General's sad tale. Mercy did not know the full story, only that he had been jilted. Certainly then, he too would have reservations about such prospects in the future. That knowledge made Mercy more comfortable for she could not stop her mind from drifting back to the praise of his pleasant features, missing leg notwithstanding.

Blast it, she thought. Such schoolgirl thoughts were unlike Mercy, who assured herself that they had only come to mind because she had had rare occasion to find herself in the company of a man who was not her brother. Still there was a calm strength to General Bradley that was apparent in his manner that somehow put Mercy at ease.

The visit was over before she knew it and Mercy was surprised to find that she did not find the afternoon unpleasant. She had not been made to participate too much in the way of polite conversation, only making the barest of comments here and there while General Bradley and Simon conversed. Yet she did not feel her contribution had been lacking. Mrs. Smith led the Baggington siblings to the door and waved them off with a promise to provide hot scones the following day.

When the door closed behind them Mercy offered her brother a scowl.

"You would have said no," he argued although she had not yet said a word.

"Of course I would have," she laughed. "I have no way of teaching a man how to sit a horse!"

"His injury can be overcome," Simon protested.

"Perhaps," she agreed. "But I have no knowledge as to that end. You cannot give him false hope, Simon. Such is the nature of these types of injuries. It is called crippling for a reason."

"Edmund refuses to be crippled by it, and why should he? He has mastered all manner of tasks in the past year that he had been told he could never do again. My goodness, Mercy, he ought to be bound to a chair. His determination has gotten him this far and I will not see him denied if a solution can be found."

"That is very optimistic," she said with a sigh.

"He is my friend."

"That does not solve the problem of how he expects to sit a horse when he cannot grasp with his legs."

"You ladies ride sidesaddle and cannot grasp," he countered.

"Are you suggesting that I ask the gentleman to switch to a lady's saddle?"

"You know that I am not," he said in a huff. "I only thought that you might have a better understanding of the balance of such since you *do* ride with *both* of your legs to only one side."

Mercy blushed. "Such talk," she murmured, for she had never heard any of her brothers refer to any part of a lady's body.

"I am sorry for my frank language, Mercy, but surely it is the same."

"It is not the same," she murmured. The carriage fell into silence, but neither of the siblings were cross. Rather, they were trapped by their own musings as they each considered the impossibilities that lay ahead. Mercy was not one for optimism. Life had taught her too soon that all roses have thorns and clouds were more likely than sunshine. All that is beautiful can be snatched away in an instant. Surely the General knew this, since he had lost his leg at war, no doubt he was whole one moment and damaged the next.

Was it not the same with her? One morning she was an innocent child, and the next she was not. She could not change her own fate, but perhaps she could help General Bradley change his.

CONTINUE READING....

The Healing Heart ~ Mercy
by Isabella Thorne

Made in the USA
Coppell, TX
16 January 2021

48319819R00146